Vices and Virtues

The University of Nottingham
Student Anthology

2016

First Published 2016

Copyright © 2016 retained by individual artists and authors

All Rights Reserved

No part of this publication may be reproduced, stored in any retrieval system, or transmitted in any form or by any means, without the prior permission in writing of the respective author nor be otherwise circulated in any form of binding or cover other than that in which it is published and without a similar condition including this condition being imposed on the subsequent purchaser.

ISBN 978-1-326-59918-8

Vices and Virtues

The University of Nottingham
School of Education

UNITED KINGDOM · CHINA · MALAYSIA

BA (Hons) Creative and Professional Writing

Supported by generous donations from Nottingham Alumni and Friends through The University of Nottingham's School of Education

2016

Acknowledgements

This thing didn't write itself! There are a lot of people who helped to create this little book, and you all deserve some serious kudos.

Firstly we would like to thank all of the tutors on the creative and professional writing course at The University of Nottingham, whose lectures and guidance have honed us as writers over the last couple of years. In particular Anthony Cropper, who provided valuable advice and help (and countless emails) when we needed it.

This anthology is dedicated in memory of David Kershaw, an inspiring and much-loved tutor who passed away in August 2015. He was the original brains behind the project and without him our ideas would still be scribbles on a whiteboard. We finished this with you in our hearts.

A big thankyou to the students on the course (are we allowed to thank ourselves?) and all the other talented writers who sent us their work. You guys rock our socks.

Lastly we would like to thank you, dear reader. We hope you enjoy *Vices and Virtues,* which has been a long time in the making. And here it is: the last annual creative writing anthology, but by no means the least!

Love,

Grace Haddon (Editor) and the CPW Anthology Squad 2016

Contents

The Colours of Sin – Greg Morrison – 1
The Wedding – Anouschka Greenwood – 3
Red Stone – Isabel Payne – 5
Harassed – Lottie Britton – 7
Heat of the Bullet – Mick Powis – 8
In The Dark – Mollie Stone – 14
I Have This Punctuality Incapability – Anouschka Greenwood – 18
The C Word – Sarah Daoud – 19
He Loves Me Not – Lottie Britton – 26
LOADING – Grace Haddon – 29
Darker Tones – Dale Cross – 33
Cold Coffee – Harry Blacker – 39
Passing Stranger – Carys Kitchin – 44
Reflected Pain – Mick Powis – 46
The Way Out – Lottie Britton – 47
Wrath – Harry Blacker – 49
Pride – Matty Kelsall – 50
Blood and Honey – Grace Haddon – 52
Dance – Carole Wilkinson – 62
Elena – Jack Adamson – 63
Who Said Three's a Crowd? – Harry Blacker – 69
Seven Heavenly Haikus – Mollie Stone – 71
A Son – Isabel Payne – 73
Epiphany – Carole Wilkinson – 78
… – Grace Haddon – 79
Patience – Matty Kelsall – 80
Cover of the Book – Carole Wilkinson – 81
The Clouds Are White Horses – Anouschka Greenwood – 88
The Inspirer – Kwaku Asafu-Agyei – 92
Meet The Crew! – 93

The Colours of Sin

Greg Morrison

We were gifted a garden, a tree lay within.
We plucked fruit from the tree, our original sin.
What followed were the sins which laid us to waste,
the vices that held us from the virtues we chased.

Envy, yellow happiness we feel for a friend,
stained red with the blood that brings friends to an end.
Envy is the orange of the longest sunset,
drawn out as the longing for what we do not have yet.

Confuse not lust for love, though similar they seem.
For love's red is tender, but lust's red, obscene.
Our heart leads us onward, pumps blood through our veins.
Driven by lust it's left empty, its efforts in vain.

Gathering gold's a fool's errand, though fools we all are,
our greed too is gold, as gold as the stars
it tempts us to reach. Still reaching, we grow old.
In death, it lays with us, our greed, our fool's gold.

Gluttony is as green as the plagues we must suffer,
as our kings and queens feast, left to starve, their own brother.
Nature's growth too is green, the plants we produce,
yet we cut down more and more for the few to consume.

What will lead us to death, what comes after the feast,
is what makes us inhuman, what likens us to beast.

The sloth is non-moving, 'tis as brown as the rust,
which leads us to death, ashes to ashes, dust to dust.

Through pride we are proud, it is white as a cloud,
it feels pure, we are sure, 'tis the sin we're allowed.
Hold not to thy pride, lest it be thy downfall.
Pride compares us to the Lord, He is mightiest of all.

Worst of all, wrath, like the night, pitch black.
It feeds on our anger, it leads our attack.
Upon our souls it is written, like commandments in stone,
give into thy wrath, thou shalt face life alone.

The Wedding

Anouschka Greenwood

If you were there, darling, you would have laughed. The flowers were in clusters of lilacs and baby pinks; grand orchids were in every corner, their elegant necks reaching high. Some lilies had opened early; their pollen littered the ground, staining the shoes of middle-class ladies in white satin heels. There were bowls of potpourri on every surface that Mrs. S had taken the liberty of going round and repeatedly spritzing with her own perfume. You would've laughed as I followed her, picking out all the stupid things like pinecones and cinnamon sticks.

If you were there, darling, you would have sighed. You'd have seen I was wearing silver not gold, ivory not blush, chiffon not lace. 'Why?' you'd have yelled, doing that thing that you do when you're angry – where you rub both eyebrows with one hand until all the little hairs face in the wrong direction. 'But money,' I'd say. 'But love,' you'd say and we'd both know you were right.

If you were there, darling, you would have cried. I used words you wouldn't have recognised as my own in a dress worth more than both of our savings combined. I'd have given you a ten pound note to wipe your tears on and you would have ripped it up in front of me.

If you were there, darling, you would've smiled as our song came on. I made it play right near the end, when the room was clearing so for 3 minutes and 22 seconds I could pretend it was you I was dancing with. My shoes were sticking to the floor and the blue and yellow strobes licked every shiny surface. I stared at them as they raced across the room faster than the beat of the music. I watched them change and move and merge into the colour of the grass we used to picnic on each June. Where you would eat all the blueberries out of my fruit salad, though they were my favourite too, where we would drink Prosecco if it were payday weekend and where we would snooze until the growing cold told us it was time to go home.

    If you were there, darling, my hand would find yours and we'd leave that place and never look back.

Red Stone

Isabel Payne

It was May 2008 and as the bright Iraqi sun shone, a small boy tried to move under the mound of sand. His name was Hakim. It meant "wise". He was six years old.

"It" had begun again. Hakim couldn't cover his ears, so squeezed his eyes closed tighter. He wanted his mother.

'Ummu,' he silently cried.

Using all his strength he raised his head, but had to let it fall. He tried several times until he was exhausted. Then the sand above him moved. He could hear voices, but couldn't understand what they were saying. Something touched his head; he heard a shout:

'Over here.' Several hands descended upon him, felt along his body; cleared away the sand. The soldiers pulled him out. He gasped for air and opened his eyes.

They were everywhere. He'd seen them before, driving the tanks that rolled along the dusty road close to his village. One of them picked him up, yet curbed his instinct to protect the frightened creature, putting him down alone further along the road.

'The kid's OK,' he said.

Hakim stared at the scene in front of him. The children's bodies lay scattered across the bloodied ground; limbs twisted; ugly dolls. He covered his eyes with his hands and howled.

He couldn't remember much before the first explosion earlier that day. Only that he was walking back from school. He was happy because Ummu didn't let him go to school every day. She often said that it was too dangerous for him to go because of the heavy fighting. Today he wanted to tell her that he'd come top of his class in counting. As usual there had only been a few children attending the class, but he'd still come top. Perhaps she'd let him have some of her home-made sweets. He loved her. She sang to him softly when he couldn't sleep and hugged him to her chest when he hurt himself. She felt warm and safe and smelled of flour and spices. Most of all he liked to finger the gold necklace she wore, stare into the deep red stone which hung from it. He had to look after Ummu now. His father had been taken away from them.

The noise started again and Hakim ran, then stopped; there were dead mothers and fathers lying along the roadside in front of him. He'd seen them like that before, but the sight never failed to haunt him. He tried not to look, but his eyes were drawn to them. He trembled. He was thirsty and tried to run on but his legs were too weak, so he knelt on all fours and crawled towards the village

When he arrived at his village the houses had disappeared. Grey smoke rose from the rubble. There was nobody left. His heart raced. 'Ummu!'

He saw beyond the debris a clump of bushes and crawled towards them. A large pit had been dug behind the bushes, fresh sand and soil piled high alongside it. He peered inside. The clothed bodies of the murdered villagers were lying there. His eyes scanned them, then he turned and shuffled away.

He didn't see it at first, thinking it merely the sand glistening from shafts of sunlight. Then he stopped. Stayed very still. It lay on the ground partly hidden under a small shrub: a gold necklace with a deep red stone. He picked it up. Its catch was broken. Clutching it tight, Hakim crawled under a bush, lay down and, with head in hands, closed his eyes.

Harassed

Lottie Britton

His hand on my thigh
I feel his breath on my neck;
He whispers softly.

His eyes are on me
I dare not look his way, fear,
Anxiety, Touch.

Pressed up against me
I feel his hand slide down low.
Open mouth, no sound.

Shifting in my seat,
Subtle strokes from a stranger
I'll never forget.

I have run for miles
In fear I'll see the face that
Still haunts my dreams.

Calling me, I turn
Lips pressed together, whistle
I raise my finger.

Heat of the Bullet
(A True Story)

Mick Powis

Saddam Hussein "got it into his head", a quote he gave to the Economist newspaper on January 4th 2007, to invade Kuwait in August 1990 to assist Kuwaiti revolutionaries. Later proven to be a front for his real agenda, which was to take control of the Kuwaiti oil fields.

10:00 am tea break. The crew room was only half full, yet their drone was deafening.

The sergeant's voice bellowed through the ageing, wall-mounted intercom. 'Powis to the office, Powis to the office.'

A strange thing must happen when corporals get promoted to sergeant, I thought. *Maybe they have voice implants to make them sound menacing and authoritative?*

I could feel the glares from colleagues penetrating to my core, I could almost hear their thoughts. *Oh aye? What's he been up to? I bet he's in trouble again*.

Of course, none of that was true. I'd kept a close eye on current events in the media. The burning oil caps in Kuwait, Iraqi tanks and soldiers crossing the border. Saddam Hussein on the front page of every tabloid and broadsheet paper. The television channels couldn't get enough of him, he was like the newest pop star to hit the scene. As for his information officer, Muhammad Saeed al-Sahhaf or *Baghdad Bob* as the Americans nicknamed him, he was a joke.

As I entered the control office, the sergeant glanced up from his paperwork. 'The boss wants to see you.'

He had a wry grin on his face, a look to say *I know something you don't.* He couldn't have been more wrong, I knew exactly what was to come. 18 months ago, I had received notification from the Ministry Of Defence. The letter stated that I had been placed on the Quick Reaction Force team, a force of manpower ready to deploy to anywhere in the world within 48 hours to deal with whatever was thrown their way. I hadn't done anything special to deserve this accolade, your service number was generated at random to make it a fair system. With the situation in the Middle East it was inevitable I would get my draft notice before long.

I knocked on the boss's door and was immediately beckoned to enter.

'Morning Powis. Have a seat young man.' I sat in the chair directly opposite him. 'I have a signal here from command, you see...'

His words faded from my hearing. I just wanted my orders. To get out of there, back to my quarters and get my kit ready for the duties that lay ahead. The boss finished his ramblings and I begged his pardon to leave. Everything was on my draft notice, travel arrangements, who to report to and so on. 21 hours and I would be on the Tristar from Brize Norton air base to Saudi Arabia. Just enough time to pack and get a few wets – pints of beer to civilians – in me before leaving.

The flight was as ordinary as it could have been under the circumstances. It was when we landed that the *fun* started. Over the intercom came the pilot's shaky voice.

'Leave all your belongings. Get off the plane and run for cover. We've landed right in the middle of a scud storm.'

The intercom clicked off and everybody cleared the plane in quick time, heading for cover. I glanced up at the sky and sure enough I saw my first scud.

The risk to us was minimal. The missiles were too high, they must have been bound for some target in Kuwait.

Even so, it certainly got my adrenalin pumping. The *all clear* siren screamed around the base with bodies emerging from every air raid shelter hideout there was. I made my way to my muster point and waited for instructions.

The brief on my detachment orders stated I was to work with the United Nations peacekeeping force. We were to assist the Red Cross with their humanitarian aid effort. They'd been doing charitable work in troubled areas of the world for tens of years, but this place was too dangerous for them to operate without an armed escort.

I listened intently as the commanding officer delivered a rallying speech which any football manager would have been proud of. At the end, he explained that we had too many forces for the task; spare troops would go about normal duties with the rest of the camp.

'If I call your name you will report to the UN quartermaster and collect your blue uniforms. The rest of you report to your respective areas of work.'

I was a 23-year-old man facing my first tour of duty in a war zone. My heart pounded as I waited to hear my name read out. It wasn't.

Fear never came into the equation. Bravado, excitement, adrenalin, they were all there by the bucket load, but not fear. The new orders from my section leader were to carry out refuelling duties on the Chinook helicopters as they ferried the infantry to and from the front line. I couldn't believe it. All this way, the chance to finally put my practice to use and I got the refuelling job.

'Chin up mate,' a voice beside me said, 'It's not as dull as it sounds. We get to go to *no man's land*. We wait for the choppers to drop off the troops at the line. They come to us to refuel, then they go back to base to collect more infantry and just keep doing round robins. Piece of cake really and no danger to us. So all's good.'

His words *no danger to us* echoed. 'I guess that's not too bad then. Well at least I can say I was here,' I chuckled to myself then went to look for my quarters.

On day two we met up again at 07:00 hours. Twenty-five personnel, ten refueller trucks and three Land Rovers with trailers. The personnel consisting of a sergeant, a corporal, three cooks and twenty refuellers. We set out in convoy to our layup point. It was an old ruined settlement with just a few crumbling walls and a watering well. We had enough rations for our two-week deployment as we set up camp and settled in.

The sergeant called, 'Stand to.'

A call that went out when we were either under attack or having an exercise. We mustered at our given areas and the *good old Sarge* came round, giving us all our arcs of fire. This was standard practice. If the shit hit the fan, we all knew what area to cover so we weren't shooting at the same target wasting ammunition. This done, we went back to our duties.

On the morning of the third day, the choppers came in thick and fast until the lunchtime lull. Which was a relief as the smell of the stew the cooks had been preparing had made me hungry. The words 'Chow down troops,' came from the mess tent and we needed no more invitation.

I had just taken my first mouthful. 'Stand to, stand to.' It was the Sarge, only this time I could tell by the tone of his voice that this was no drill. I gathered my hard hat and SLR rifle and went to my defensive position, *stag point*. The SLR, self-loading rifle, had been the weapon of choice in the British forces since the early 1950s and had proven its worth in many conflicts.

Turned out to be just another of the sergeant's drills. No enemy, no attack, just our lunch going cold.

'Just a reminder, lads. Don't let your guard down; it could happen for real at any moment.'

He was a proper old school drill sergeant who liked to keep us on our toes. As the next couple of days also went by without incident, I was beginning to think that perhaps this duty would be a doddle after all.

Day three started pretty much the same, the first refuel was due in at 06:30 and right on time four thirsty Chinooks arrived. Within 25 minutes they were serviced and off on their way.

'Right then boys. I reckon we have about 40 minutes till the next lot get in so I suggest you get a brew and breakfast.'

I couldn't help chuckling as I thought about the sergeant being *all heart*. The first I knew of an attack was the sound of the enemies' AK47 assault rifle. Its distinctive *clack, clack, clack* could be heard in the distance followed by the high-pitched fizz and whoosh sounds as the rounds flew past, ricocheting off the derelict buildings.

Over the sand dunes came a hoard of insurgents, some on foot, some in technical, the 4x4 pick-up trucks converted into fighting machines by adding a 50 Cal machine gun. I held my position, crouching behind a small stone wall just to the right of my arc of fire. Five, six, maybe more. I didn't stop to count, I just selected target after target and double tapped the trigger. One fell, then another. I wasn't sure if I'd hit them or if they had dived for cover. I wasn't bothered, I kept shooting. I made sure to count the rounds as I fired.

The last thing you want to hear is a blank click as your magazine runs empty. The SLR mag held 20 bullets so after 9 engagements you change mags. Leaving one bullet in the chamber for emergencies and one in the mag for later. The enemy advance was progressing well, their attack growing in ferocity. The thud of the 50 Cal joining the noise of the AK. I ducked down to re-load.

The extreme fiery pain coursing through my body was tremendous, the like of which I had never experienced before and never wanted to again. To say it was like a red hot poker being slowly inserted would be an understatement. I'd been hit! I could think of nothing but the pain. They go through drills in training, but all that information is lost when it actually happens. I remember rolling in agony, thinking it would go away. As much as I try, even now, I am unable to recall much from this point, till waking in the field hospital.

The surgeon explained how lucky I was. It had apparently been a 7.62 ml round from an AK 47 (Kalashnikov) that had ricocheted and lodged between my fifth and sixth rib. *Lucky* kept going through my head. Lucky for who? Not for me, that was sure. I was later told that one of my colleagues, who had been in my stag point, had suffered worse than I. His was fatal. So I guess the surgeon was right. I never went back to my post. I was flown back to the UK as a casualty of war. After 2 weeks of recuperation I was back at work. Back to normal. Just a physical and mental scar to remind me.

In The Dark

Mollie Stone

When it goes dark I turn into a psychopath. Usually the psychotic episodes are fairly contained but on 24th October I didn't quite catch it in time. I was sitting in my black chair at my desk, in my small student room at university. Next Monday was mine and Tom's four-year anniversary, so I decided I was going to be all cute and make him a gift. I got a new deck of cards and wrote something that I loved about him on each card. Fifty-two things. The last card read, "you never gave up on me". We hadn't had it easy the last few weeks; lots of arguing and frustrated messages were sent and received. I was content that my idea would solve everything and I spent the next three hours adoring him.

Tom had gone to an open mic that night; he was studying at a university further north in Leeds, a popular music degree, he was an extremely talented guitarist. I had spoken to him earlier in the evening and I was just about keeping my jealousy in check, as he was to be performing with a girl he was studying with. After my hours of work on his present, I realised I hadn't received a reply to my earlier message. I tried to ring him and I was sent to answer phone. I had a better relationship with his answerphone than him. I sent a few more text messages, the psycho in me bubbling up as I started to question where he was and what he was up to. As an insecure person I worried for his safety but doubt of his honesty was creeping in, there wasn't an ounce of trust between us.

An hour dragged by and I finally got a call back.
'Hey Lexi.'
'Hi. Where are you?'

'I'm just walking back to the flat.'
'Only just? It's 12 o'clock, where have you been?'
'I've been with Jess.'
'Who the fuck is Jess?'
'The girl from my course, we were just jamming and chatting in her room–'
'And you didn't think that would be weird?'
'We were just chilling.'
'I haven't heard from you for the last four hours Tom. And now you're telling me it's because you were "hanging out" with some other girl? Was anyone else there?'
'No it was just us, why do you overreact to everything?'
'Overreact? I don't know how you dare say that after what you've put me through tonight.'
Beep.
'Oh for fuck's sake.'
That is when the psycho well and truly took over. Tom's phone had died, so I was left reeling at the fact my boyfriend had spent the evening with another girl and didn't think he should tell me about it. Bastard. So I messaged him again and again. Nothing. I got Facebook up on my laptop and started searching through Tom's recently added friends. Jessica Michael. Found her. So then without a second thought I messaged her.
'Hi Jessica, I'm Tom's girlfriend. He told me he was with you tonight. I can't get hold of him, is he still with you?'
Enter. Then I wondered whether I should have done that. Too late.
'Hi, yeah he was with me but he left about 15 minutes ago. His phone was dying when he left x'
Fuck off with your "x". So I pretty much knew his phone had died. For the next twenty minutes it was just tapping fingers and pacing. I eventually got a notification on my laptop that Tom wanted to FaceTime.

His puffy, red, alcohol-fuelled face came onto my screen, he looked cross with me. How could he possibly be cross with me? Then it started. The usual words struck me, crazy, psycho, bitch, and I retaliated with emotional blackmail. It went quiet, we had both exhausted all the swear words we knew, and the realisation came of what was about to happen.

'I can't do this anymore.'

Tears blurred my vision. I felt like my heart had hit the floor.

'Do what?'

'You know what. It's over Lex.'

'No… No you can't just do that. I have spent the whole night writing out reasons I love you Tom. No, you can't do this. No.'

All I could see was brown hair and I could hear the faint whimpers of him crying, his tears soaked up by the hoodie I got him last Christmas.

'I'm sorry Lexi.'

I flew back from my chair. Hands in my hair, a gasp of air drawn sharply to fill the sudden gaping hole. All I had thought about for the last four years was him. Tom, Tom, Tom, Tom. What was I going to do? To the bathroom.

'Lexi where are you?'

His voice forcing its way into my ears as I stood pressing scissors hard into my left wrist. Stupid girl, I was ready to end it over a prick that didn't even have the balls to finish it to my face. Stupid girl. I went back to the laptop and slammed it shut. Panting and alone, I suddenly heard Hannah and Danielle banging on my door, the flatmates I'd only met a few weeks before. They cared more than the boy I thought I loved.

'Lexi? Are you okay?'

Tom had messaged Hannah telling her what had happened. Do it from eighty miles away and let someone else clean up your mess.

I stood facing the mirror; the only colour left in my face was the black stalactites of mascara and an expression that simply portrayed emptiness.

I Have This Punctuality Incapability

Anouschka Greenwood

I think my body clock is failing me
cause if I'm just fifteen minutes late
that's on time for me.

It may seem like irresponsibility
but I swear on my life
my alarm is mocking me

I have to turn it off, it's hurting me –
I tell myself that by not sticking to these "rules"
I'm sticking it to the bourgeoisie

and I would attempt at being early
but if I start now I probably won't
get round to it till February.

I know I have to change this mentality
but waking up at the crack of dawn
with a smile just doesn't come naturally

And I blame the woman who gave life to me;
even then I was two weeks late
I guess I've always meant to be

walking in the footprints of society
constantly.

The C Word

Sarah Daoud

Tommy Moyes was a mathematician with a penchant for dispelling well-known beliefs about arithmetic. At the age of 29, after four years of research he had proven that $1 + 1$ did not in fact equal 2 but 3. This discovery had propelled him to mind-blowing heights of global fame and earned him accolade after accolade in the field of numbers. It had also earned him death threats from all around the world as people struggled to make sense of life after Tommy's revelation made them question everything they'd ever known about maths.

Quicker than you or I could say algebra, Tommy bought himself a ginormous house in the country now that he was famous and irrevocably wealthy. He decked it out with the latest types of security including an American ex-wrestler called PM Skunk and over the years he began to acquire the types of things he felt were fitting for a rich man to own. Such as the world's first hoverboard, a pet dolphin, a page from the original copy of the New Testament, insurance on his eyes, a wife called Kandi, an item of clothing from every designer brand in the world, Fiji, a space in Elvis Presley's family burial plot and diamond encrusted underpants (a good idea at the time of purchase...).

Now at 46 and onto his fifth wife (the seventh removed cousin of Oliver Cromwell), Tommy had made numerous shocking discoveries and completely overhauled the education system's teaching methods of those dastardly digits, but this wasn't enough. Because there was one thing he had not managed to obtain in all his years of being infamous and filthy rich. Revenge. Revenge on the creative arts and anyone associated with it. You see, Tommy came from a long succession of creatively-minded people, and his parents (an actress and a theatre director) hoped that he and his three older siblings would stay true to their heritage of creative genius.

Becky had had her debut novel, *The Book of Fabrication*, printed in 136 languages before the age of seventeen, Michelle had won an Oscar for best supporting actress at twelve and Pete was making a name for himself as a sculptor by ten. But Tommy... oh dear...

Tommy could not fathom the arts. He simply couldn't get his head around anything creative. His parents told him it was OK, his talents lay elsewhere, but Tommy refused to accept this. He too wanted to have something to show off about at family gatherings and so he convinced his parents to take him to the doctor, who referred him to a specialist, who referred him to a world-renowned specialist who confirmed Tommy's worst fear. He didn't have a creative bone in his body. Tommy was crushed.

He shut himself away in his bedroom, determined to prove everybody wrong. Two and a half weeks later he emerged, his eyes red, clumps of hair missing from his head, his clothes on backwards, faeces smeared on the wall behind him spelling out "once upon a" and a pungent smell emanating from him. His parents had stepped back in horror. 'Numbers!' he'd said, grinning like a baboon at them, 'I love numbers!' Yes, at nine years old, Tommy had discovered that numbers were his friend, cold and factual, they understood him and he them. Finally, he knew his place in the world!

As Tommy learned of his mathematical prowess, he began to spend less time with his family, preferring to be with other math boffins, most of them over twenty years older than Tommy. Perhaps it was during conversations with his fellow math maniacs that Tommy began to believe that the arts were a pointless blight on the world, or maybe it was the horrified expression on Ringo Starr's face during a backstage meet and greet when he turned to Tommy and asked him what sort of music he liked and Tommy replied with 'I prefer maths.' Or maybe it was when Michelle made a joke about him being the black sheep in her family whilst accepting a BAFTA for Best Actress in a film about the true story of a sheep going on a murderous rampage after being rejected by its herd. Whatever it was, by his late teens, Tommy detested the arts and wanted nothing to do with anyone who thought opposite. Hence his decision to cut off his family and change his last name from Hoyes to Moyes.

When not ruining the world population's general knowledge of maths, Tommy spent his time concocting plans to destroy the dreams of those who aspired to harness their creativity into a career. It had taken him years and years of dedication but finally... he'd managed to think up an idea. It was perhaps the most creative thing he'd ever done. A simple idea, it involved utilising the TV channel that he'd bought a year ago and renamed Channel 1+1. So far it only aired news broadcasts about numbers and a version of Countdown that didn't include the bits that involved letters. Tommy had decided to add a reality show to the channel and this was where his plans of revenge came in. The show would be called *Arts Island*. The concept would involve dumping a load of creatives on the island under the pretence that they were competing to complete their various projects in the space of three weeks whilst having to undergo grisly tasks. The supposed prize was to be £50,000 for funding their latest work.

Everything was in place. An obscure island had been erected in the middle of an ocean somewhere. Five contestants had been selected after an audition procedure that Tommy had attended. He'd planned to pick the five that irritated him the most. The first contestant was a jewellery maker and had seemingly adorned herself in every piece of jewellery she'd ever made. She'd rattled and jangled her way through the interview and Tommy had had to leave the room for a moment, forcing himself to take deep breaths. Then had come a film editor, who after bouncing into the room clutching a can of Red Bull in one hand and a cigarette in the other had talked extensively about watching Godzilla as a child and falling in love with film and sure he was an editor right now but one day he'd be a director because at the moment he was just honing his craft, you know? Throughout this, he'd constantly pushed his large black lensless glasses back up his nose, at one point accidentally poking himself in the eye. The casting agent working with Tommy had looked at him questioningly and Tommy had nodded tightly, yes… the film editor was in. Next was a website designer. Tommy had stared disdainfully at the bearded man's faded Slipknot hoodie, baggy denim shorts and flip flops. The man was a walking identity crisis and before he'd even spoken Tommy had barked 'You're through' to him.

'Who's next?' asked Tommy, after the website designer had wandered out of the room.

'Nova Sunshine… erm, she's a mime artist,' said the casting agent.

'Oh God,' said Tommy, his voice cracking a little, his glasses misting up.

'And then we have a novelist,' said the agent brightly.

Tommy choked back a sob. 'Just put them both through. Then send the rest away. I'm going home'.

He muttered the words to Ten Green Bottles under his breath during the car journey, starting from 1000. Once home, he locked himself in the Numbers Room where he watched a documentary about how the first number was invented. It helped calm his nerves.

The five contestants and their families had all signed contracts that included small print which waived all rights to sue should injuries or worse occur as a result of anything Channel 1+1 had seemingly no control over. Such as a hurricane...

The contestants arrived on the camera-infested island in high spirits, thrilled at such an opportunity and excited to meet one another. Their first task was to build tree houses for themselves and they got straight onto it, delving into the supplies provided. Tommy watched from the channel's new studio in an annexe on his property. The producer, a mousy man with a protruding nose and permanent twitch under his right eye, stood by anxiously. He wasn't sure how Tommy had managed to hoodwink him into working on the show. But it certainly didn't involve the £100,000 he'd been promised. Tommy sat in a leather chair, his eyes narrowed at the various screens in front of him that showed different shots of the island.

'What's the plan tomorrow?' he asked the producer.

'They'll have to search the island for their individual work spaces.'

'The day after that?'

'After a breakfast of the placenta of a goat, there will be a game of dare or dare. The public will decide which dare was the most creative and there'll be a prize for it. Later in the day they shall have to catch as many flies as possible which they'll prepare for dinner.'

'Hmm. What time is the hurricane predicted to hit?'

'Around one in the morning,' said the producer.

'I'll be back to see their fate. If there're any problems, let my PA know.' Tommy strode out of the studio, leaving the little mouse to get back to work.

The next two days passed by slowly for Tommy despite his best efforts to distract himself with his latest project, turning the entire 2 times table upside down. But finally… it was here. The night of the hurricane. Tommy paced the floor of the studio, a team of lackeys trying not to get in his way. The producer stood by, thinking of what he'd been told to say when any concerned members of the public rang. 'We are assessing how safe it is to send in help…' The twitch under his eye was the worst it had ever been.

Tommy had barely slept the night before, so immense was his glee. He hadn't watched any of the show so far, not interested in wasting his time on such piffle but ratings were phenomenal and millions had voted for the dare or dare task. The show was doing well. Irrelevant of course. All that mattered to Tommy was that he'd be able to rid the planet of a few of these arty farty people. After that… who knew? Run in the next election perhaps. Become prime minister and set in place even bigger plans to diminish creativity wherever he could. Maybe in schools and universities…

A wind blew menacingly on the island; trees rocked side to side, the sea rose in furious arcs. The five contestants huddled together at the base of a tree. The mime artist turned to the closest camera. She waved, moving her hand side to side in an exaggerated waving motion before scratching her head, raising her eyebrows and turning her palms up to the sky, her shoulders practically touching her ears. The camera, hanging from a branch, was suddenly hit by a gust of wind and thrown to the ground. Tommy sniggered to himself.

An hour and a half later, the hurricane had gathered momentum and Tommy had disconnected the phones, citing they were ruining his viewing pleasure. The contestants, still hoping help was coming, had scattered in search of shelter. Two of them hadn't been seen for 30 minutes. Tommy sat on the edge of his chair; he could barely wait for it to be over so a body count could be conducted.

The producer had headphones and a perplexed face on. 'What?' said Tommy, noticing. 'What is it?' He stood and grabbed the headphones. After listening for a moment, his eyes widened. 'Find the voice!' he barked. People scrabbled to do as he said. A moment later, a camera was on the novelist, hiding in a cave a few metres above the sea that had been swelling steadily for a while now. 'Zoom in!' commanded Tommy. His face lost all colour. 'Becky!' he whispered. He gaped. How did this happen? His sister was a contestant?

The producer looked at Tommy, waiting for further instruction. Tommy thought back to his childhood. Becky had always been his favourite sibling. Older than him by seven years, she had often been the one to read him a bedtime story when their parents were too busy or at a function. He'd never told her that he didn't find the books interesting. She had been the only one who'd listened carefully to him when he'd enthused about numbers, even though she didn't understand most of what he said. When he'd gathered his family and told them he wanted nothing further to do with them, she had been the only one he hadn't looked in the eye.

'Tommy!' she was screaming. 'Tommy, I know you're watching this, help me!'

Had she been following his career and life all this time? Had she got on the show to be close to him again?

'Mr Moyes?' said the producer. 'Should we help her?' The water was in the cave, it had reached Becky's ankles. Tommy turned away from the camera, yanking the headphones off and throwing them to the ground.

'No,' he said. And that was that.

He Loves Me Not

Lottie Britton

11.45
    Still no sign of Ben. I walk down the stairs into the kitchen, feeling the cold tiles beneath my feet. I switch on the light, making me wince. As I make my way towards the kettle, I notice Ben's dishes from last night in the sink. Hasn't done them then. I stare disgusted at the dried cheese and tomato on the plate. Bloody dishes. This is what it has come to, me analysing Ben's dirty dishes.
    Why hasn't he called? Why is he so late? My head throbs as I start to question everything. I flick the kettle on to drown out my thoughts.

12.00
    Midnight. I stare over my mug, watching the milk swirl around and gradually mix in with the tea. I let the steam warm my face and inhale deeply, trying to relax. I pull my phone out of my dressing gown. One message from Ben.
    'I'll be home late. Don't wait up.'
    Typical. I reach into my other pocket and pull out a box of pills. I pour the remains of my tea onto Ben's dishes, letting it trickle down the drain. I grab the bottle of wine I have hidden at the back of the cupboard and let myself drop back into my chair.

12.30
    Two glasses of wine and a pill, I don't feel a thing.

This is what Ben has turned me into, a 44-year-old woman drinking herself to sleep every night. I hate him for that. I start to gnaw at my fingers, peeling bits of skin right off until they are raw. I pour myself another glass.

1.00

'*You left your dishes in the sink again,*' I text back.

No reply. I swallow another pill, it scratches my throat.

'Let's play a little game Ben,' I say aloud as if he can hear me. 'For every unanswered message, I'll take a pill. Ready?'

'*I know you're not at work, you bastard. I'm not stupid.*'

Pill.

1.30

'*Working late? What's her name this time?*'

Pill.

1.45

'*I can't do this right now Julia, I'm in a meeting. We'll talk later.*' Ben finally replies.

I swallow more wine. 'Meeting.' I mutter.

2.00

I take the remaining four pills out of the box and arrange them in a circle, like the petals of a flower. I pick up the first one and swallow it down with some wine.

'He loves me.' I remember the first time he told me he loved me. I was sitting on the bed anxiously waiting for him to get back from work, excited to tell him the news. As he came through the door, I jumped into his arms and wrapped myself around him. I handed him the pregnancy test. Speechless, he hugged me and whispered three simple words, 'I love you.'

'He loves me not.' I swallow the second pill. The late nights started after I lost the baby. He blamed me. I feel as though he loved that baby more than he ever loved me. We didn't talk anymore. I didn't deal with it well, wine became my lover. There were nights Ben would come home to me passed out on the sofa.

'He loves me.'

Pill.

'*We'll get through this*.' His words echo in my head and I feel dizzy. I drink more wine and pour the last of the bottle into my glass. After helping me get sober, things were looking up. Two months I'd been without a drink. Ben was more focused on me than his work, we spent more time together. I was happy again and I love him for that. I didn't think that would ever be possible. Then the paranoia set in.

'He loves me not.' I pick up the last pill and swallow it quickly. I close my eyes and the room spins.

I never used to have trust issues until Aureja. Ben worked with her for two years until finally it happened. He begged me not to leave, and swore it would never happen again. I didn't believe him, but I stayed anyway. The paranoia got worse and I began drinking again.

My phone buzzes and I try to focus my eyes on the message.

'*I can't do this anymore Julia.*'

He loves me not.

LOADING

Grace Haddon

People tend to think that apocalypses are loud, messy things.
    Floods sweep away whole continents, aliens beam down and blow us all up, mutant killer frogs rain down from the sky. Take your pick. If you can imagine it then it's probably been made into a low-budget film somewhere.
    In reality, finishing us all off doesn't require anything quite so elaborate.
    This apocalypse starts on a Friday night, as all the best apocalypses do.
    Picture Nigel, your average guy at the start of the weekend. It's the end of a long day, and his girlfriend Tina is having a night out with her friends. What does your average guy do in such a situation? He starts up his laptop, turns on inPrivate browsing and settles down to watch some porn. Soon enough, a busty blonde is about to do something unspeakable with a cucumber.
    And then she stops.
    Nigel is confused. He clicks a few times, but she isn't budging. Then a little circle appears in the centre of the video, conveniently covering up what dignity she still has. Above this appears one word.
    LOADING
    Nigel rolls his eyes.
    And waits.
    The video doesn't load. Sighing, he clicks (with his left hand) to another video, but nothing happens. The screen has frozen and even the loading wheel isn't spinning anymore.

In the end Nigel gives up and wanders into the kitchen in search of baked beans, which isn't going to help his libido. When he comes back the blonde is still there, unmoving. In frustration he holds down the power button to shut down his laptop.

Nothing happens.

It slowly dawns on Nigel that his computer might be frozen indefinitely. Tina will be home in just a few hours. Will the blonde still be there when she returns?

He closes the lid and tries not to think about it.

Elsewhere in the world, Katie in California is typing a text to her boyfriend. They never spend time together, she tells him. He's always watching football with his mates, or working late. They need to talk. Perhaps it's time they went their separate ways. With tears in her eyes, she presses *send*.

And she waits.

The message is still sending.

It soon becomes apparent that this phenomenon is happening all over the world. The internet is down. And so are mobile phones, radios, TVs and iPods. Anything with a screen is now endlessly loading.

Nigel's porn is indeed still frozen when Tina comes home. He hides his laptop away and prays that she doesn't need to check her Facebook tonight.

He isn't alone in his struggles. Kevin is experiencing inner torment because his PlayStation has frozen and he can't get all of his *Skyrim* trophies. Lauren can't catch up with *Orange is the New Black* on Netflix and now her life is devoid of meaning. And spare a thought for Louise, whose Instagram of her haloumi salad with grated carrot might have elevated the internet to a new level of jealousy. Or possibly not.

It is said that if you deprive any civilisation of three meals there will be anarchy. But deprive the human race of technology for more than three minutes, and you get insanity. Like all the best apocalypses, people start to go bananas.

With no sign of light at the end of the loading screen, riots flood the streets. People suggest faulty satellites, or data-freezing ionisation in the air, but no one has the answers. Everyone starts to lose their minds.

What is the world to do? There is no Facebook, no email, no TV or Tumblr or Tinder. Everywhere, on every screen, there are egg timers and blue donuts of doom. There's no telling how long this will last for, or even if it will ever end. For a while there is only confusion and despair.

But then the human race does what it does best. It adapts.

There is no email, but there is still the postal service – which is soon staggering from the weight of so many letters that it has to triple its staff. There are no news channels so people have to rely on paper aeroplanes and word of mouth. Before long, women's magazines display articles such as *Which Loading Symbol Are You? Customise To Match Your Personality!* And *Your Loading Screen And You: Exercises To Pass The Time*. Laptops and iPods become buried inside drawers and cupboards.

Katie is delighted when her boyfriend laments the lack of football on TV. They start having nights in, with boxes of takeaway noodles.

Without his video games, Kevin has no excuse not to meet up with his friends anymore. He discovers that the *Dungeons and Dragons* board game is almost as good as *Skyrim,* though he's a little disappointed there aren't any large-breasted orcs. His friends tell him to use his imagination.

So as it turns out, the apocalypse isn't such a big deal after all. They still have art galleries and takeaways and annoying kids on bikes. Essentially, the world is still the same. Humanity has fought and survived. Communication is more difficult, but at least Sat Navs have become slightly more useful now that they've stopped working entirely. People talk to each other more, without screens separating them. They have adapted, survived, and perhaps even improved.

And then one day, the internet is back. Technology that has been gathering dust suddenly flickers into life. Video games resume, recipes load on webpages.

Katie sees her text beginning to send, telling her boyfriend that she's through with him and that they have no future.

Smiling, she presses *cancel.*

Kevin's *Skyrim* game resumes but he doesn't notice. He's too busy designing a new character to play in their *Dungeons and Dragons* game. It took him a long time to create: it's a large-breasted orc.

One by one, the world decides that it was better off without so many buttons and screens. Technology had begun to enslave them, filling their days with wasted time. And they decided that, for the most part, it wasn't wanted anymore.

It's an apocalypse that the world embraced, and was much happier for it.

Even Nigel. After struggling to make do with dirty magazines, he was eventually forced to admit that his girlfriend Tina is a lot better than the fake stuff he used to watch on the internet. Even if she isn't quite as flexible.

Tina doesn't see it this way when she hears strange noises coming from their bedroom, and rediscovers Nigel's laptop buried at the bottom of his sock drawer.

Darker Tones

Dale Cross

I can still remember, after so many years, when I would create such divine masterpieces. These now-withered hands could never again create such vivid beauty. My art, which the mortals below have named "Rainbows", were my life, my purpose for being. I remember taking the red out of roses, watching the garnet petals fade to a snowflake white. Where else did you think white roses came from? I would borrow yellow from the flesh of a lemon and weave it with red to create a vibrant orange. Pink, from the leaves of cherry blossom trees. Green, from the towering trees of dense forests. Purple I would snatch away from a resounding bolt of lightning and finally blue, from the depths of an iceberg core. Once all the finest forms of each colour were gathered in my grasp, then and only then, would I begin to paint on my canvas.

    My siblings and I were sent here from beyond the stars, not knowing our destination, only knowledge of a single purpose. To please. I would often wonder if they had found a place to please as easily I had. The mortals dubbed this particular patch of land, in the middle of a vast ocean, as Fallcreathe. It sat there like a tiny blemish on this pure blue surface, surrounded by sheer cliffs. It had vast amounts of open grasslands, a few forests made up of various plant life, and at its very centre a single town. It was not a busy town, but a place where everyone knew everyone and there was always an open door for anyone who needed it. I made this place my home and my purpose for being.

The eyes below would wonder at my creations, never knowing of the hand that cast such marvellous scenes. Alas, such beauty is fickle. For mere moments I would share in watching the colours fall and fade like smoke on a hasty breeze. All my hard work, gone in a matter of seconds. But was all my hard work worth the effort? Of course it was. To see the mortals' eyes stare in amazement at colours so readily available to them made me smile. All it took was an artist's hand to bring them to life.

Every day I quested for new samples, searching for ever-richer colours than before. Crystals became my gambit. This world is abundant with rocks and minerals varying in such a wealth of shades and colours. Violet amethysts, azure sapphires, auburn ambers, all such wonderful and inspiring gems. Only once was I able to create a Rainbow consisting of colours harvested from gemstones alone. The stones are rare and desired so greatly by the mortals; it is difficult to acquire some for myself. It used to be hard for me to watch the colour drain away from something so treasured by mortals and yet so menial to me. Of course, I keep a select few for myself. Some are just too strange to simply discard or harvest for colour, but I often wonder about what colour I could draw forth from them.

On my tenth journey, delving deep into the nearby mine rich with these stones, I found something. Whilst flitting around in the deeper quarters, I found a radiant silver stone riddled with string-thin veins of red. It protruded from the tip of a lone stalagmite, pulsing like a heartbeat, getting louder the nearer I encroached.

The pale light briefly illuminated the room's surface, pulsing in time with the thumps. It was as though it had been placed there, as if it wanted to be picked up, but this item did not belong to this planet. Even from where I stood, I could feel a dark aura radiating from it. Never had I come across something so peculiar.

This stone could hold properties this world wasn't ready for and could be dangerous if it were to fall into the hands of the mortals, so I plucked it from its perch. Something at the back of my mind derived so many questions about the stone's origin, and yet my curiosity and lust for perfection clouded my judgment. Without intention, the light drained instantly into my palm, leaving me with blank stone as grey as a storm cloud. My veins felt as though they filled with fire, spreading just as quickly, then suddenly my vision began to fade and I fell into darkness.

I'm not sure how long I remained unconscious, laying there in darkness, but the sound of mortal voices reaching this far down the mine was a decent enough indicator. Like a time-forgotten machine grinding to life, my mind awoke. I swept along under cover of darkness and left the mine behind me. I climbed and climbed until suddenly the sunlight pierced my eyes, but as my vision slowly adapted and I peered at my shielding hand, words failed.

My hands had changed, resembling the peculiar crystal I found before I fell unconscious. I felt no pain, but as I examined my hand, I could see the red veins, the same as the crystal's, weaving into my skin, spreading.

Weeks passed and the disfiguration spread. More than half my body had altered to become a deathly grey, littered with a web of crimson veins. At first, I panicked and searched through every book I had that could provide me with a solution, but slowly my concern began to ease. In the time it had taken me to search I had felt no pain or discomfort, and despite the visual change I was myself. I decided to let fate see what would become of me.

I had failed to create a masterpiece since the incident and my urge to do so was scratching at the back of my mind. If I was going to die, I wanted to see the mortals' awestruck faces one last time.

I set off on what might have been my final search for the purest of colours, but what I found was something else. At the bottom of the cliff lay one of the mortals that worked the tavern next to the mine. I had seen her numerous times, handing out flagons of ale with a glistening white smile surrounded by a set of plump pink lips. Her hair was usually a bright golden yellow, but there she lay in a puddle of cherry liquid. In fact, the more I examined her decaying corpse, she could easily be a Rainbow herself.

All of the colours were there. The pool of redness and strands of butter hair, those signature pink lips and the sickly green skin. How could I have been so blind? The mortals had all the colours I could possibly need, in such a variety of shades, too. I scooped the fluid into one of the vials attached to my belt, picked up the mortal and returned to my home.

I carefully placed the gaudy corpse on my table and began to harvest. The peach lips unveiled a deathly blue, embedded in a mass of violet bruises; she was dead and yet so full of life. The liquid I collected was richer than any garnet or ruby I ever found in that mine, but I needed more. The red primarily leaked from her eyes and so I began there, only to reveal eyes greener than her dying flesh. As I dissected further, I could see my skin progress quicker and quicker. Red veins overlapped and laced together like crashing waves.

By the time I had finished harvesting, my body was entirely converted. Not a single shred of my previous form remained and yet still I felt no pain. I turned to see my reflection and stared at the mass of grey, riddled with a garnet web of veins, standing before me. What had I become? I looked at the mortal husk. All those fermenting colours, slowly getting richer with age, gone. She was empty, blank... I needed more. The scratching at the back door of my mind was growing louder like fingernails clawing at a chalkboard. I had to get those colours, one way or another.

My first targets were the mortals that dared to venture too deep into the mine. Oh, how easy it was to pick them off, one at a time. A quick snuff of a miner's candle light and the smell of a smoking wick would fill the pitch-black air. One final horror-filled shriek, abruptly cut off. Then silence.

They kept coming down there, bringing more men to guard the miners. They began to carry weapons when a "wicked beast made of coal" was seen skittering out of the mine. Nevertheless, in darkness the mortals are blind.

Eventually, fifty-three bodies lined my wall. I arranged them in order of their colours. From the first ones that had begun to darken and swell with carbuncle abscesses, to the fresher ones that had hardly gained any colour at all. In a way they were a Rainbow in themselves. I was ready to make my final creation.

I ascended into the heavens and gathered my pallet together. Red of the mortals' blood, blue of their suffocated lips, yellow from their rotting flesh, all blending together in the palm of my hand. I looked down to see the mortals below gathering at the cliff's edge, watching me, the so-called "monster". The colours swirled and mixed until I released them into the sky below me, and I watched them bleed through the clouds to form a technicolour arch, a vivid mirage... A masterpiece.

As I watched, the faces of the dead mortals bulged from within the colours, surfacing to moan with torment before sinking below the glowing blankets. Their gaunt mouths gaped beneath hollowed eyes, and the occasional withered hand reached out, grasping for an escape.

The mortals below screamed and wept. Maybe they recognised a loved one, but no matter.

Look at my masterpiece and bask in its glory. Maybe one of you will have the honour of sacrificing a vial of crimson blood, a limb turned green from decay, or an eye turned grey from death, and when I turn this world into an alabaster canvas, I'll find another planet with mortals worthy of my power and do it all. Over. Again.

Cold Coffee

Harry Blacker

Paul woke to the sunshine coming in through the gap in his pale curtains. He promptly sat up, swung his legs round, and planted his bare feet on the floor. The bottom of his blue and white striped pyjamas hovered above the grey carpet, exposing his bony ankles. He crinkled his nose and squinted at the bright morning sun before taking one big gulp from the glass of water on his bedside table. He stood and walked over to the corner of his room, sliding on his slippers.

In the kitchen he sat at a small square table and ate dry cornflakes out of a clean white bowl. He drank coconut milk out of a plain white mug. For five minutes he sat in the same spot and stared ahead out of the kitchen window, counting the birds that flew by. Then he stood, washed up, showered and put on brown corduroy trousers and a clean-ironed chequered shirt, tucking it in and leaving the top button undone.

He combed the small amount of hair on his head, picked up his keys and wallet, and walked out the front door.

After a seven-and-a-half minute journey he arrived at The Lemon Tree, and as usual stood outside looking in for approximately three minutes. The outside furniture was set up under the sunshine and on the far left table sat a tired woman drinking a large black coffee. By her feet lay a bulldog, lapping up water from a shallow bowl. Through the window he could see it was not too busy, only a couple in the corner eating breakfast and a young mother with her baby by the window. It was only 8:57.

As his wristwatch turned 9:00 he gently pushed open the door, hearing the 'ding' of the bell above him. Behind the front counter a woman was bent slightly, scribbling something down on a small scrap of paper. On hearing the door she snapped her head up and beamed at Paul. A few strands of hair that had come loose from her messy bun fell over her blue eyes. Blowing them back with the corner of her mouth, she called across the room, 'Morning!'

Paul's fingers began to shake lightly, tapping against his leg, his breathing was shallow. 'G-good morning.' He tipped his head slightly and tried to muster a smile through his trembling lips.

'Beautiful day today isn't it? Warm too.' She hummed a little, her fair pink lips pursed. 'Latte as always? Sit wherever you like, I'll bring it to you in just a moment.'

'Thank you.' Paul quietly sat down in the usual uncomfortable wooden chair that faced the counter. He was still, watching her potter about frothing milk and grinding coffee beans. She was small; small and sweet. Her bare face wore no make-up and no lines, her eyes soft and young.

As she moved out from behind the counter with a drink in hand, Paul's breathing jarred. Her pale thin legs were in a floral skirt that swished with her movement, her flat chest hidden behind a strappy white t-shirt. She placed the coffee in front of him, smiling.

'Here you go, let me know if you need anything else.' She crinkled her nose. As she walked away Paul kept still, watching her as she disappeared into the back room. He looked down at his coffee and gave it a little stir, then put his hands on his lap and waited for her to come back out again.

He bit his lip as his breath deepened, growing hot under his trousers. He tapped his thighs and squeezed his eyes shut.

She came back out, holding three clean spotted mugs that she stacked upon the coffee machine. Placing a strand of hair behind her ear, she started cleaning the counter surface while her lips moved in time with the Katy Perry song that played in the background.

Paul rubbed his hands together underneath the table and shook his leg aggressively, gritting his teeth and gulping several times a minute.

She reached up and pulled her hair loose. Paul averted his eyes, looking down at his untouched coffee. He reached his bony fingers up and pulled down on his neck, digging his nails in and muttering to himself, 'Stop it.'

It is still quiet, the mother and child have left. Only Paul and the couple remain in the shop. An older woman with short red hair and dark clothes speaks to the girl, gives her a cloth and a small bucket of water then disappears again. She walks round the counter and begins cleaning the table legs, bent down on the floor.

After a moment Paul thrusts his chair back with such strength it creates a screeching noise along the floor and startles her. He attempts an apology but instead walks quickly towards the bathroom in the corner of the shop. She carries on cleaning.

She stops and shuffles behind the counter when a young man walks in with his son. After ordering a slice of carrot cake and a small chocolate milkshake, they sit by the window behind Paul's empty chair. Once Paul comes back out from the bathroom, he sits and picks up his latte, touching the rim against his old chapped lips. Cold.

*

The sunshine woke me up today. The streaming sun through my curtains reminds me of her hair. It always does. I touch myself in the shower again, feeling the warm water trickle down my legs; the comfort of her mouth on my neck is washed away like the cornflake dust in my bowl.

The route is the same. Along the brick wall with the dying flowers at its foot, through the narrow alley shrouded in trees, along the edge of the park.

Three minutes in, I stop and sit on a bench facing the concrete path that cuts the grass in half. I sit for half a minute, watching them walk by. Three girls, identical clothes, linked arms as if to support each other. Giggling and gossiping, short skirts and ripped tights. The one with short brown hair looks at me, smiles innocently and carries on. I feel her small shoulders between mine, her black chipped fingernails on my thighs, her strawberry-flavoured breath in my ear.

It is eight minutes past nine. There is still steam rising from my coffee. She comes out from the back room and potters about as usual. I can feel her skirt in front of me, on my lap, running the fabric between by fingers and tracing the outline of the patterned flowers, her thighs exposed. Her tiny hips and small frame, a pair of childlike white pants sitting below her t-shirt. Beneath her pants it is smooth and soft, pale and new. I feel a little sick. I throw her skirt and her pants on the floor but nothing is there. I look up and she is the same as before, sorting cups, moving cake, cleaning counters, clothes on.

I no longer see steam from my coffee, just the white frothy centre and darker brown rim. It will merely be warm now, but I don't mind.

Suddenly she is in front of me, on the floor. Bent over. Her t-shirt has fallen forward, just slightly. Perfect young breasts upon her untouched naked body, the crevice in her neck and the warmth upon her skin. My fingers around the lukewarm mug in front of me feel like her breasts, gripping tightly I imagine her small erect nipples hard in my palms.

I can feel the heat emanating from between her legs. Her thighs feel like caramel under my worn hands, when I touch her the heat on my fingertips surpasses that of my coffee. With my hand I cause her small chest to rise and fall, as her breathing gets heavy her pink lips part.

I am in the bathroom. I can feel my trousers tighten. The door is locked. I undo the button and zip with haste, pulling the toilet seat down I sit and face the door. She is in front of me, she does not resist. I don't have long. I can feel myself, moving heavy to the beat of her milky stainless heart. The tips of her hair are delicate on my shoulders; their touch follows the rhythm of our bodies.

I am in the bathroom, on my own. My hand is wet and she is not here. I lean back for a moment, look up at the swirls of plaster on the ceiling. Maybe when she's older, eight years or so – but then I won't want her anymore...

I clean up, zip up, stand up and walk out.

On the way to my seat I notice a young boy sipping a chocolate drink. His father is reading *The Times,* pretending to listen to him talk about dogs. I sit down and look up at her.

I touch the rim of my coffee to my dry lips. Cold.

Passing Stranger

Carys Kitchin

'Spare change please?' Derek, a homeless man in his forties, pulls the old sleeping bag closer to him as he sits in the doorway of the closed city centre travel agent's. Partygoers walk by without paying attention to him. Too busy with their own celebrations. Fireworks go off in the distance, partially lighting up the night sky.

Laura hurries by, stopping to check the time on her phone. 22.36. Sweeping her long blonde hair out of her face and readjusting her gold dress.

'Spare change please?' Laura hears as the crowds pass. She looks at Derek, checks the time and walks over to him. Almost tripping on the crack in the pavement.

'Whoops,' she says to herself. Crouching down next to Derek, she looks at him. 'Are you ok? Have you got anywhere to go tonight?'

He looks at her and looks around the doorway that he's made his home for the night. 'Yeah sure, going to check in to the Hilton soon.'

Unsure if he's saying it as a joke or making fun of her, she laughs nervously and goes through her bag. Getting two £10 notes out. Reaching out to pass them to him.

'Here, take it, get some food.'

Derek shoos her away with his hand. Angry at the thought of it. 'I'm not a charity case, I'm not going to be a project you can throw Daddy's money at in order to make yourself feel like a good person.'

Shocked by his comments, Laura places the money back in her bag and walks off round the corner.

'Sorry,' Derek says under his breath as he watches her walk away.

Minutes later, the sound of heels becomes louder as Laura approaches Derek again. A full plastic bag in her hand and a smile on her face. Laura sits next to Derek in the doorway.

'Right, I hope you like chips,' Laura says as she hands a packet to Derek.

Derek looks down in shame. Sighing, combing his hand through his greasy hair. 'I'm so sorry. I shouldn't have said what I did,' he says as he looks up and faces Laura. She places a hand on his shoulder.

'It's in the past,' she says as she hands him the bag of chips and a plastic fork. Derek quickly tucks into his food as Laura checks her phone.

'You should be out bringing in the New Year with friends,' he says, 'not here on your own.'

'Neither should you'. Laura writes down an address on a piece of paper, and hands it to Derek. 'This is a homeless shelter. They'll take care of you tonight. Don't be on your own.'

As Laura stands up and readjusts her dress, she hands the money to Derek. Placing it in his hand and closing his fist.

'Be safe,' she says as she smiles and walks off towards the music of the clubs.

Reflected Pain

Mick Powis

There again, watching.
Judging me, mocking.
Not understanding.
He doesn't know me.
How could he?
Seeing the outside, with
no access to my head,
my thoughts that trouble.
I know what he's thinking.
Look at your size,
the plate,
food spilling over.

I will consume it all.
But that's not the end,
that will come later.
The bathroom.
He doesn't have to see.
Averted eyes.
Not him, he gloats.
I could break him
but others witness.
Do I break them all?
The mirrors.
None to judge
or ridicule.
Pain destroyed.
Free.

The Way Out

Lottie Britton

I tug at the door handle, once. Twice. It won't open. I start to panic, making the door shake but it won't budge.

'Tim,' I whisper.

'Tim, the door won't open, I think we're locked in.'

Silence. I run my hand along the wall and flick the switch, lighting up the emptiness of the room. I stare at the shape of our bodies still pressed into the sheets, like footprints on wet sand.

I walk over to our bed and brush the duvet, feeling the warmth of where I lay moments ago. I look over at Tim's nightstand and notice all his things have gone. Maybe he's left for work already? I glance at the clock I got him last Christmas. 6:02.

I climb back under the covers and sit up against the headboard. I look at Tim's side of the bed, puzzled. I notice a small scrap of paper hiding between the pillows and grab it.

I hope you can understand why I've done this.

I leap up and try the door again, making it rattle. I bang my fist against it over and over until I can't feel my hand anymore, leaving it red and bruised.

'Tim please. Let me out!' I shout through the door.

I get my phone out and dial his number. He answers on the second ring, probably expecting a call.

'What are you playing at, let me out! Why are you doing this?'

'I know what you did Natalie.' His voice is oddly calm.

I feel the heat rise to my face.

'What are–'

'Don't try and deny it. John told me himself.'
'Tim look it was just once…'
'I don't care. I can't live like this anymore.'
'I know you're upset but you can't just leave me in here. When are you coming home?'
'I'm not. I'm on my way to my parents' house now. It's what's best for the both of us.'
'No it's not, I know we can get through this. We've both made mistakes.'
'I'm not talking about you. It's what's best for me and Sam. Or hadn't you noticed something was missing?'
'What…'

He hangs up before I can finish. My heart starts pounding harder, making my head throb. This can't be happening. I rush to the other side of the room and stop. Slowly, I approach the cot. I stare at the space where Sam once lay, a small silver key in his place. Beside it is a small note.

We've both been trapped in for too long. We need to get out before we hurt anyone else. It's time to face the truth Natalie. I have. Now it's your turn. T.

Wrath

Harry Blacker

Like the flick of a
broken switch
surrounded by peeling wallpaper
smudged dust and
bleeding soil –
the sweet sugar
is now
salt in scars
on the tip of your tongue.

Perplexed,
a muddle of thoughts –
the cream was smooth
the switch flicked
your skin has curdled
and it's there on the surface
for everyone to see.
Broken,
just like the door.

Pride

Matty Kelsall

To me you're meek, and I can never be wrong,
and I make you weak so that I seem strong.
You hold to hope, and you pull me through,
you make me cope, as I turn from you.

I look for another, as you look up to me
while I set to smother your want to be free.
Then I make you meek so I can never be wrong
and I make you weak so that I seem strong.

I need to be held but will never say why,
I'd rather live the hell than expose the lie.
I'd crumble in myself as reality gleams,
as stripped of my wealth I'm all that I seem.

But you open my mind and I bring you in
But in time you find the extent of my sins.
So I make you meek, so I can never be wrong
and I make you weak so that I seem strong.

With your hand to hold and tears on your shoulder
I can risk being bold and brave growing older
but I tear you down, and I keep you there,.
To keep you around as something to wear.

Your hopes and dreams, set aside for me
show the extremes of the man I can be,
as I keep you meek so I can never be wrong
and I make you weak so that I seem strong.

And once you leave, it's you that I'll blame
and I'll never believe you'll ever be the same.
That I pushed you aside, and my choice was made
and your love died as I walked away.

But your hope returns, and I grow strange
And my mind burns as I hide from the pain.
"You were always meek. I was never wrong."
I'll remember you weak and tell myself I'm strong.

Blood and Honey

Grace Haddon

The rain swirled through the open door like a cloud of angry insects as Harold shouldered it open then wiped his feet meticulously on the doormat. His funeral suit was drenched a darker shade of black, but now he was home he smiled as he trudged into the kitchen to dump the bouquet of lilies. The flowers peeked out of the bin, perfuming the air with their corpse-like scent.

Harold wandered into the living room. Already it seemed eerily quiet without her. Fog pressed smoky hands against the French windows, casting strange shadows over the furniture. Harold drew the curtains, then went upstairs to get changed.

The books were the first to go.

They landed with a satisfying thud as he threw them in, the box juddering with every impact. *Beginner's Guide to Beekeeping, Keeping Bees in the City, To Bee or Not To Bee?* Each carried a snippet of her smooth, sing-song voice.

'Did you know that bees don't sleep? They just go still in the night.'

Thud.

'At least try to show some interest, Harold. Why must you always so touchy about it?'

Thud. Thud. In they all went, little pieces of her existence, well-thumbed and sticky. He swept them off their shelves until the box wouldn't hold any more.

Spots of darkness spattered the carpet as rain battered the window. Harold looked up. He'd been sitting in her room for almost an hour and he hadn't even finished clearing the shelves.

This room had once been the study. When they first moved in he'd planned to use it as such, anyway. But within just a few days Elaine had filled it with her books and equipment, determined to make the most of their larger garden. That had been nearly forty years ago, and now it was a minefield of spare jars and dusty boxes.

'It's called living, Harold. Most people actually don't mind having a little mess in the house. If it bothers you so much, don't come in.'

And so he hadn't, not until now. Finally, he could bring some order to the place. He'd show her how a house *should* be run.

Harold lugged the box downstairs. It would take a day or two to clear the room. And a can of grey paint. He'd never understood her obsession with yellow. She'd probably thought it was *quaint.*

As he passed the kitchen he caught the smell of something rotting. The lilies were already withering, the spotted white petals turning brown. He squashed them down with his fist until the bin flap closed again. Elaine's friends from the beekeeping group had adorned her grave with sunflowers. They'd looked far too cheerful on the freshly-turned soil.

Harold froze as there was a tap, tap, tapping at the window.

A bee flew repeatedly against the glass, its wings a blur as its furry body sought a means of escape. The tapping sounded like human fingernails. It must have come in through the window and been trapped by the blinds.

The angry buzzing set his teeth on edge. Elaine had found the noise peaceful, but it triggered something in Harold. Perhaps it was some vestigial fear from when he was stung as a child. Perhaps it was something more primitive than that. But the sound sent invisible insects crawling under his skin. Thirty-five years of living with them hadn't changed that.

Their marriage had never been perfect, even when they'd first moved in together. However, it wasn't until she'd joined that beekeeping club that Elaine had become truly insufferable. She would prattle endlessly about bee-friendly plants and queen cages and hive tools. Occasionally she had brought one of her bee friends round, and Harold would always make the point of speaking to them as little as possible. Elaine still found ways to irritate him.

'I saw my first drone yesterday,' she'd said one afternoon, sipping her tea with honey – never with sugar, of course.

'Ooh! You're lucky,' said her friend enviously.

'Well, they don't really do much do they? The males, I mean.' Elaine leant back in her chair. 'They don't work, can't sting, and once they mate with the queen they die from the exertion.' They both laughed, but Harold didn't miss her glance towards him, the thoughtfulness in her eyes. 'There's not much point to them, to be honest.'

That was when he decided to kill her.

Harold paused in his pacing and turned to the window. The rain was building towards a downpour, blotting out the remnants of the afternoon light. He had a sudden, urgent desire to remove all trace of Elaine, anything to suggest that she had ever lived here. And he knew where to start.

It took him a while to find the key to the shed. Elaine could never keep track of anything, and she didn't like him going in. Harold hadn't seen inside it for at least six years. He finally found it under the tea caddy. Despite the rust on the key, the door opened silently.

There wasn't a speck of dust in sight. Jars covered every inch of the shelves, arranged with near-mathematical precision. It was like stepping into a jewel cave. His scowling face glared back at him from the hexagonal jars; rows of seething Harolds trapped in Elaine's cold confines.

Harold took a jar from the shelf. It was surprisingly heavy in his hand. Once the shed had been to store his tools in, but over the years she'd insisted on more space for her "spare produce" which she never had a mind to sell, and so he'd been forced to move his things to the cupboard under the stairs. This was the one space of hers that wasn't cluttered, but surgically neat. It was as if she'd spent so many years polishing jars and making labels and arranging them so neatly out of spite, as if she'd known he would one day come here and see the jewels of her life's fixation gleaming back at him.

The sight of so much honey made his teeth ache. He'd never liked it, with its cloying smell and sickly taste. Who'd had the bright idea to eat it in the first place?

It was a question that Elaine would have been happy to answer. He wondered what she'd say if she knew he was standing in her most treasured secret place, where even her husband was forbidden to go.

The lid bit into his fingers as Harold's grip tightened on the jar. The bees had always come first. Elaine had put more effort into maintaining her colony than she had their marriage. *'At least the bees don't ask me where I'm going every time I step outside!'* she'd snap.

Harold flung the jar to the floor. It broke into two pieces and the contents of her life dribbled between the floorboards. He swiped his arm along the shelves, the crashes deafening as the glass jars shattered on top of each other.

'Each bee produces about one twelfth of a teaspoon in its lifetime.' He wondered how many bees' lives were now wasted and smiled. It was like making up for the wasted years they'd spent together. One by one they went,

smashed and crashed and shattered. Those that didn't break on impact he stamped into submission under his shoes.

Then something stabbed his foot like a small dagger. Harold cried out and looked down. A large piece of glass protruded from the sole of his shoe, slimy and sticky. He swore and cursed and hobbled back to the house, trailing blood and honey over the wet grass. The sky had turned the colour of dirty dishwater as the rain continued to pelt down.

The house was dark as he returned but Harold didn't turn the lights on. He never did if he could help it; there was always the electricity bill to think about. He took some sheets of kitchen paper and limped through the house, his foot throbbing at every step. He could feel the glass moving inside the wound, like scissors slowly worrying it deeper.

The living room was bathed in grey light, but the figure on the sofa was white, startlingly white against the muted surroundings. The head was dark and swollen to twice its normal size, the skin sagging and shiny.

Harold stumbled backwards and yelled as the glass embedded itself deeper in his foot. It was Elaine's beekeeping suit, arranged over the seat of the sofa. In all the years she'd used it, there had never been so much as a grass stain on it. Except for that one smear of red on its head.

Harold leaned heavily against the arm, taking deep breaths. He'd brought it down earlier along with the rest of her bee things. It had often given him a turn when he opened the wardrobe, and it had always seemed two sizes too big for her slender frame.

It was how he'd always remember her: striding through the garden in that baggy old suit whilst the bees swirled around her. The dense black netting hid her face from view as she tended to them, and at those times he'd often thought the suit looked empty, hanging from her body like flesh from old bones.

Harold folded down the head so he wouldn't have to look at it. An empty suit was nothing to be afraid of, but it unnerved him that he'd unconsciously placed it on the side of the sofa where Elaine preferred to sit.

Harold tutted as he sat down and saw the spots of blood on the floor. Elaine had always nagged him about getting the carpet replaced but he'd insisted it was too expensive.

Blood was difficult to get out of fabrics. He knew that better than most.

The glass didn't come out cleanly. The honey made it difficult to get a good grip, and the sharp edges sliced his hands as he wrapped it in kitchen paper and pulled it slowly out of the wound. It came out stained pink, and shreds of wet skin clung to it. A final goodbye present from Elaine. He pressed a wad of paper against the wound to slow the bleeding.

The cardboard box of books sat beside him, and it had left a square of dust on the sofa. He moved it to the floor, tutting. The book that had been wobbling on the top of the pile slid off and landed on the carpet, open on the most-used page. Like all of Elaine's books it was covered in her characteristic scrawl, which had grown untidier as her hands had become unsteady with age. She'd drawn a circle around a passage: "*...and in Aegean mythology bees were seen as sacred insects, bridging the gap between our world and the Underworld.*"

Harold snorted and glanced at the cover, *The Honeybee and Mythology: a Series of Essays*, then threw it back into the box. Elaine would never admit it, but he knew she'd believed in all the silly superstitions. If one of the buzzing creatures ever got into the house she would exclaim delightedly, '*Oh, we're going to have some good luck today,*

Harold!' or *'Don't kill it Harold, they won't like that.'* She'd often spoken of the bees as if they were her family. When Harold's uncle had died a few years ago, she'd insisted on telling the bees. When her sister had had a baby, even when the neighbour's dog had been hit by a car, the first thing she'd done was to rush into the garden to tell her bloody bees.

Harold glared at the dishevelled suit and thought of all the years he'd imagined doing this. Now he had one final task to do. One last thing and she would be truly gone.

It was right at the bottom of the garden, and a long walk across the marshy lawn. A little wooden house with no windows, turning black in the rain. Elaine's pride and joy. He'd forbidden her to get one, but that hadn't stopped her.

Harold prowled closer, swinging the hammer at his side. If the hive was smashed the bees would swarm and sting. But today it was raining, and even he knew that the beasts couldn't fly if their wings were wet.

He raised the hammer above his head, then hesitated. Elaine had given so much of her life to these bees. A more pretentious man might have said she lived on in them. The hive was the temple at which she worshipped. To destroy it was an act of desecration.

Then he remembered Elaine's snide smile as she compared him to a drone.

The rain seemed to shiver as he swung the hammer into the hive with all his strength. A circular dent appeared in the weathered wooden planks.

'She's dead,' he snarled as he brought the hammer down again. The hive was robust, but the damp wood couldn't hold out forever. 'No one to protect you nasty little buggers anymore. Should have done this years ago.' He imagined he could hear Elaine's horrified protests as he smashed it, a low wail under the hissing of the rain. His clothes were soaked and the neighbours would think he was a madman but he didn't care. This had been a long time in coming. Now he was free. He had won in the end.

The wood dented under the onslaught, but it refused to break. As his arm began to ache he realised he couldn't hear any angered buzzing. He unfastened the lid and slowly lifted it up, wondering if the rain would flood the hive and kill them that way.

Harold pulled back the lid.

The hive was empty.

The honeycomb was there between the wooden panels, but there were no insects scuttling over them. The hive was silent, as if they'd all just decided to fly off. It was something Elaine had constantly fretted about: if the queen was dying, sometimes the bees decided to leave and find a new home. It was called swarming.

With a shiver, Harold turned and walked back towards the house. The hive had been left open when Elaine died. He'd seen the bees then, as they crawled over her suit whilst she lay unmoving. The doctor said she must have slipped and hit her head on the corner of the hive. He'd agreed that it was the only possible explanation.

Harold had thought about it often enough, how to do it so it would look like an accident. Even so, it had taken a few days for the shock to wear off. He'd found himself drifting aimlessly, unable to come to terms with the sudden silence of the house, unsure what to do with his newfound freedom.

Like bees without a queen.

The phrase popped into his head unbidden. He'd been listening to his wife too often, but Harold didn't believe in ghosts.

The empty hive was still on his mind as he limped back inside, leaving his shoes by the door. He felt weary from enduring so many condolences, from having to be so damn miserable all day. It had taken all of his concentration to maintain a sombre expression, to smile bravely whenever someone said his name. It was almost seven o'clock but it might as well have been midnight from how dark it was inside. He wasn't even sure if he could be bothered to go back upstairs. Instead he slumped down on the sofa again. He wouldn't admit to feeling afraid or guilty, but he didn't want to sleep in that bed tonight.

Harold closed his eyes, glad that the day was finally over. He listened to the rain as it tap, tap, tapped against the window like a hundred tiny fingers, whispering for him to sleep.

He didn't remember when he fell asleep, but suddenly the tapping had stopped. He opened his eyes to darkness, with only the faint traces of daylight casting watery shadows across the carpet. He winced at the pains in his back. As he stretched, his foot nudged the box of books. He glanced to one side and stared blankly at the bare arm of the sofa for nearly half a minute before he realised what was missing.

Harold straightened up slowly. He sifted through everything he'd done yesterday, trying to remember when he'd moved it. But he only remembered leaving it on the arm of the sofa.

He stood up and opened the curtains.

It was early morning; the fog had dissipated although the garden was still cloaked in shadow. But there was no mistaking the white figure crouching by the hive.

Harold leaned closer to the glass, not daring to breathe in case it misted the view and the figure disappeared. The arms were buried in the open hive, as though it was looking for something. Or waiting for someone. He stared at it for a long time but it didn't move. He couldn't see the face.

The tapping was quiet at first. Little pattering fingertips beating out a rhythm, but as it grew in volume it became faster, more insistent, until it sounded like a hailstorm. And no matter how much Harold stared up at the sky, he couldn't see a single drop of rain.

'Enough of this,' he muttered. Then he bellowed at the window, 'Enough of this!' Elaine was dead, of course she was. Either someone was messing around, or –

Harold picked up the hammer. Then he strode over to the living room door.

He noticed the thrumming vibrations in the door handle the moment before he opened it, but by then it was too late. They came around the door, fluttering and scuttling and singing to him. An army of glittering eyes and black legs.

They flew to him like long-lost children, eager for reunion. They landed on every inch of him and enveloped him in a living, buzzing blanket.

Harold kicked and stamped and shouted for help, but they crawled onto his tongue and marched down his throat. He swallowed some in his panic and they wriggled and stung inside him. Dozens of tiny feet crept in his ears until he couldn't hear his own screams over their grating voices.

Harold turned towards the garden and could just make out the blur of white in the distance. It seemed to beckon to him as he squinted at it. Spots of black appeared in front of his eyes, and they spun and grew larger and larger as the bees enveloped him, crawling over his bubbling, sweating, weeping skin. He closed his eyes against the onslaught, his body still twitching as they crawled around inside him. The buzzing grew to a roaring crescendo as the bees rejoiced in their victory.

The swarm had found their new home.

Dance

Carole Wilkinson

She sits, alone.
The memory of her dance
still lingers in my mind.
Each, movement, enchanting.
Just out of reach.
All longing to touch.
Oblivious to my stare,
slender hand, stroking her glass.
The rhythmic movement, enticing.
Red wine staining her lips,
full, begging to be kissed.
Elegant lace mesmerising
as legs gracefully cross.
Image of my hand, caressing her thigh,
the contours of her body.
Passions rising.
A private dance.
As it wraps around her
does she sense my longing?
Is this the spur to dance again?
Or the lure of the ten dollar bills
we greedily thrust.

Elena

Jack Adamson

'Hello, is anyone there?' Elena whispered to the dim corridor. The fluorescent light strips flickered and hummed. The droning drilled itself into her skull. She heaved, the stench of damp and human waste catching in the back of her throat.

I need to get outside, I need to get outside was the only thought that flashed in her mind.

Pushing herself from the floor, she staggered down the hallway. The flashing light above Elena's head flickered brightly enough for her to see the door to flat 248 was ajar. There was a body prone on the floor.

'Tom? Tom!' Elena rolled the body face-up.

'Jesus, fuck!' Tom was barely recognisable. Something had torn his lower jaw from his head; his face was etched in an eternal scream. Elena felt bile rising in her throat.

Sitting back on her heels, she covered her face with her hands, sobbing.

The door behind her clicked shut. She didn't stir, tears squeezing out of her closed eyes. A hand held her shoulder. She leant her head against it, comforted by the touch.

A second hand grabbed her chin, forcing Elena to look up. Its face was humanoid but the jaw was too wide, grinning rows of dark teeth. The hand on her shoulder had gone. An elongated finger, rough from the crusting of dried blood, brushed her fringe from her face.

Cocking its head to the side in a jerky motion, it slowly pushed the finger into Elena's eye, squeezing fluid and blood out of the socket.

*

After placing another cardboard box onto her living room floor, Elena stood up. Hands on her hips, she surveyed the new apartment. As she stepped into the kitchen to make a drink, the phone on the side began to ring. Sliding her finger across the screen, she answered.

'Hey babe, I was just checking that you had moved in ok?'

'Hi. Yeah it's been fine, though I'd have preferred it if you had been here to help.' Elena straightened out the new wedding band on her finger as she spoke.

'I know, I would have liked to be there as well but you know how much of a hassle this job has been recently. Have you met any of your neighbours yet?'

The kettle clicked off.

'Not yet, but I have only been in the building for a couple of hours.'

'Ah, right. Well, I'm going to love you and leave you, as I need to get back to this meeting.'

'Ok, text me when you're done. Love you.'

'Love you too.'

Elena put the phone back on the counter. *Happily married is fucking shit.*

A knocking at the door roused Elena from her daydream. Opening the door she was met by a young man, maybe a few years older than her.

'Hi, I'm Tom. I'm guessing you are the new neighbour?'

'Hi, yes, I'm Elena. Which flat are you in?'

'I'm in 248. And before I forget, I got you this as a house-warming gift.' He brandished a bottle of wine in Elena's direction.

'Thank you very much. Would you like to come in?'

'That would be lovely.'

He followed Elena back into the kitchen.

'The kettle has just boiled, but do you want to crack open this bottle of wine?'

'That sounds like a grand idea. So where have you moved from?'

Elena poured out two glasses. 'Quite a small place: up North, though you probably haven't heard of it.'

'Fair enough. Could I ask why you have moved down?'

'Yeah, my husband recently got a promotion, but we had to move down here for it. What do you do?'

'Is your husband in?' Tom broke Elena's eye contact to glance around the room.

'No. He's out working, as ever.' Elena drained her glass. *Cheap supermarket shit.*

'Are you ok?' Tom spluttered, clearly shocked at the pace that Elena finished her wine.

'Hmm? Yeah, nothing I won't be able to get over.' She placed her glass on a nearby box, her thumb playing with the uncomfortable rings on her finger.

Tom watched her over the top of his glass.

Flena paused, rapped her fingers on her thigh. 'I have an idea of how to get over it.'

Tom placed his glass onto the side. 'What are you thinking?'

She slid her rings from her finger, and kissed him. 'This.'

*

Groaning, Elena tried to push herself up, looking for the light switch. *That was a fucking weird dream*. Her hands moved up to rub her eyes awake. Blinding pain shot through her skull. Fingers lightly traced the scabs that had crusted over what remained of her right eye. As her left eye became adapted to the dark around her, Elena began making out shapes; she was still in 248, though Tom's body was gone.

Elena pushed herself into a seated position, fighting the nausea that laced her pounding head. *I have to get out of here, before that thing returns*.

Elena pushed herself from the floor, steadying herself against the wall. She spat, trying to clear the last of the vomit in her mouth, the odour of stomach acid rising in her nostrils.

The humming of the fluorescent lights got louder as she stumbled back into the corridor, adding a constant drone that made the back of her head ache. Keeping her hand on the wall for support, Elena began walking to the staircase.

Fucking hell, not now. The banister was the only thing left of the staircase, the rest a heap of rubble three floors below. *It's too high to jump down, how else can I get downstairs?*

Elena began to walk back down the corridor, hoping that the stairs on the other side of the building would still be intact. Reaching her hand to the wall, her foot brushed a tangle of wire. *I'll use this, and rappel down to the first floor.* Elena took the coil of wire, tying one end to the iron girder that used to hold part of the staircase, and threw it down into the space below her.

It even reaches all the way. She edged along the girder, careful not to knock the hooped wire down. Slowly, she lowered her weight onto the wire, and slid off the girder. *At least it holds me.*

Elena started to descend, passing the dark corridor of the second floor. *Halfway there.* Moving her right hand to grasp the wire below her left, she swayed slightly and grabbed the wire. Pain shot up her arm; blood squeezed out from her right fist. Unpeeling her palm from the wire, she saw the knot that tied the length of the wire to the barbed wire, and the barb that she stabbed herself on.

A creaking above her head signalled that the wire would not hold her much longer. *I need to hurry up.*

Feeling her heart pumping adrenalin into her blood stream, she pulled the sleeves of her cardigan down; she balled the material in her palms and continued the descent. With more light coming from the first floor, Elena could see that the barbed wire had also been tied to a shorter section of razor wire. *Fuck that, it'll cut my hands to shit. I can make the jump.*

Elena began to swing on the wire, trying to make a clear drop to a flat piece of rubble. Letting go, she saw where Tom's body had been moved to: it was suspended with barbed wire below the light strip in the corridor of the first floor.

She hit the floor, knees buckling beneath her. Dust rose around her. The floor shook and collapsed, the rubble breaking through the stairs on the first floor. Elena hit the floor. Broken pieces of brick covered her lower half and red dust rose as a cloud around her.

Elena rolled onto her side and cleared the bricks off her legs. Rising into a low crouch, she saw the door leading onto the street outside. Heart pumping, she stood. Stepping off the rubble, Elena started to amble towards the door.

A click made her stop in her tracks. Then a whispering sound of metal sliding over stone.

A blinding pain shot up her legs and Elena was strung upside down, rocking back and forth, suspended by a barbed wire trap.

Through the tears that misted her vision, she saw a dark shadow detach itself from the wall by the staircase and walk towards her. Its jerky movements mirrored the way it had acted before.

Reaching its finger towards Elena's face, the face pulled back into a mocking grin. Elena felt the fingernail on her left eyelid of her eye, pain shooting out as it meticulously pushed the finger into the socket, twisting it deep into her skull.

Before she passed out from pain, Elena heard it step away from her and slide something metal from the floor. It grabbed her arms, forcing them against her body. With its free hand, it began wrapping razor wire around her, pinning her arms against her stomach. It stepped away again.

Feeling pressure on her shoulder she tensed her jaw, her mouth drying. A sharp pain raced up her body. She felt herself being pushed up. The pressure became too much and pain blazed through her. She felt something being forced up her body, entering in the space between her neck and her collarbone.

The creature stepped back, its head cocked to the side. Elena was barely recognizable; her face covered in dried blood, jaw pulled from her face, her body mummified in barbed and razor wire. A pool of blood had formed below her; the metal stake stabbed into her had drained the body of blood. A grin spread across its face. It was pleased with the result.

Who Said Three's a Crowd?

Harry Blacker

Light finger tipped touches
on the small of my back.

Her hand moves up and his moves down.

Wet lips tracing the crevice of my neck
in tandem with the
weight of her body pressed
firmly into
mine.
His palm on my stomach and
fingers through my hair
she laps at my belly button
like it's sweet sticky honey on
the back of a spoon.
I can feel him pulse in
my left hand
hard
rippling waves.
I tug
on her hair – long
soft in the creases of my knuckles.
The back of her head breathes deep
with my hips;
soft noises and quiet moans
muffled
by salty skin and hard
nipples.
We move together till my knees

are pressed deep into the sheets, I
scrape my nails down her thighs
painting pictures
into freshly spread butter icing.
She tastes like cake, a
sweet pie –
fresh out the oven;
warm, dripping.
I salivate and taste and feel
his hands gripping my hips
hard.
Scraping my teeth and biting down on
the flesh that keeps the
bones of her fingers warm.

The indented markings of a triangle
stretching out in a bid to reach the three tethered angles –
fingers, tongues and touches; we
bend and mend and form one.

Seven Heavenly Haikus

Mollie Stone

Chastity:
White is the colour
That comes to mind with her so
Innocent and pure

Temperance:
To keep up restraint
In adverse situations
Is the work of him

Charity:
Her pockets were full
His empty but he still smiles
For she is happy

Diligence:
Determination
Perseverance, diligence
Conscientiousness

Forgiveness:
Letting go is hard
When the hurt is consuming
We must all forgive

Kindness:
I really like you
The boy said to the girl
From then they were friends

Humility:
"You are so modest"
They said as the brunette blushed
Holding the gold cup

A Son

Isabel Payne

Peter and Susan held hands, having stood in line to watch the landing. The senior officers stood to attention when Mark's comrades appeared, heads bowed, to escort him from the plane. Susan closed her eyes knowing that the convoy drew closer, then leant against Peter as she sensed it pass in front of her.

It was a warm summer evening in 2011 and in the village hall Mark's farewell party was in full swing. The sounds of music and laughter could be heard along the lane. It was a fabulous night with "Good Luck" banners, lots of booze and a chocolate fountain, centrepiece of the massive buffet bursting forth like molten lava. At midnight, the inevitable conga line cascaded out onto the village green then returned to the hall where they said goodbye to Mark.

The next day there he was, their only child, now a soldier, smart and spruce, ready to leave with a reluctant kiss and a promise to write. Mark opened the front door. Susan could not hold back the tears. He turned back then and hugged her, saying, 'Don't cry Mum,' and stepped outside. Not liking goodbyes, he had refused a lift to the airport. He walked down the garden path and got into the taxi without looking back.

In the weeks that followed, they listened every night for news from the war zone. Mark wrote but only described the beauty of the desert and the camaraderie of his fellow soldiers. Peter spent long hours either digging in the garden or alone in his shed with a cigarette. Susan had the same dream most nights – a blast and then Mark falling.

'Susan, you need to get out more or you'll make yourself ill,' her friend Maggie said as they sat together in their favourite café. 'I've started voluntary work at St David's Hospital and I love it. You get to meet all sorts, you know.'

Susan pulled a face. 'I've never thought of doing anything like that. What do you have to do?'

'It's a case of taking round newspapers and sweets for the in-patients to buy. I chat and joke with them. It brightens up their day.'

Susan shrugged. 'I don't think I could do that. I detest hospitals. You're right though, I need to do something. So does Peter. He sits in the shed for hours.'

'Didn't you both used to do a lot of walking?' Maggie had not given up.

'Yes. Mark came too when he was younger. He used to like hurling stones into the sea.'

Maggie smiled. 'Well, there's a walking group advertised in the post office window...'

Peter and Susan were at the beach café the following Sunday to meet the local ramblers. They started to walk with them every week.

'I'd forgotten how good walking can be,' Susan said as they stood on the ridge looking down on the Northumbrian coastline.

Peter breathed deeply. 'It makes you glad to be alive doesn't it?' Then he felt a tap on his shoulder.

'Any idea when Mark will be back?' It was Julie Green, a college pal of Mark's. 'We're having a Christmas Ball at the college. It would be nice to see him there.'

Peter grinned at her. 'I'll mention it to him the next time I write. He'll be flattered to know that you've been thinking about him.'

'I've had second thoughts about St David's – I start next week,' Susan said, when she next met Maggie.

Maggie smiled at her. 'I'm glad, Susan. I think you'll like it.'

Susan was surprised how much she did enjoy it. She discovered that some of the patients never had any visitors, so made a point of talking to them each time she was there. She would work over Christmas. She did not like to think of these patients feeling lonely over the festive season.

It was early November when they got Mark's letter.

Susan rushed into the garden to find Peter. 'He'll be home for Christmas!'

'We'd better get a real Christmas tree then,' he said. Mark loved the smell of pine needles. He grinned.

'Julie will be pleased if he turns up at their Christmas Ball.'

On the 10th December 2011, it was Susan who heard the car draw up outside. She watched as two men in uniform emerged. 'Peter!'

He rushed to the living room. She pointed to the men walking up the path. 'The officer's eyes...'

Neither of them moved. Until they heard the knock at the door. Her eyes closed.

When Peter opened the door, he knew immediately.

'Peter James?' the elder man enquired. Peter led them into the living room.

Susan had not moved.

'I think it would be better if we all sat down,' said the Colonel, having made the introductions. Then he began the rehearsed delivery, tempered with sympathy. His younger colleague remained silent, head bowed. Peter heard,

'A brave soldier... on foot patrol... in Helmand Province... came under small arms fire.'

Susan screamed, just once, and fell to her knees.

Peter found the whisky bottle and poured them each a dram. He said nothing, just handed her the glass. He drank his straight down then Susan followed, gasping at the warmth of the spirit. Her eyes darted around the room.

'I can't stay in here – let's walk to the beach.'

'Are you sure?'

'Yes. I need fresh air.'

The beach was a murky grey. Nevertheless, people strolled along the hard damp sand, arm in arm, stood and looked out to sea. Susan and Peter walked towards it, oblivious to the activity, until they reached the edge.

'I... I didn't want him to join up... you know that don't you?' Susan looked out at the ocean as she spoke.

'Susan, don't do this,' he sighed, 'it was his choice.'

'You should have stopped him!' she cried, and turned to walk away.

Peter stood quite still, and for the first time looked around him at the winter landscape. Then, picking up a small stone, hurled it out to sea.

He found her in the beach café, a pot of tea in front of her. Just like any other customer, taking refuge from the cold sea air.

As he sat down, she looked up at him and said, 'He wouldn't have wanted us to be unhappy together at Christmas would he?'

Peter took her hands in his. 'No darling. Mark wouldn't have wanted us to be unhappy together ever. And... and he knew that this could happen...'

Her fingers tightened in his hands. 'When he said, "Don't cry Mum" as he left, I didn't think he meant only for that day.'

Susan had worked hard at the hospital in the run up to Christmas.

'You've done a brilliant job keeping the patients buoyant so far. Perhaps when the time is right you might consider a more permanent role?' said Sister Thomas. Susan was stunned at the compliment. She loved the work.

When they had stopped for lunch on the walk the following Sunday, Julie said, 'I've spoken to Mark's college friends and tutors and they'd like to make the Christmas Ball a tribute to him. How do you feel about that?'

Peter smiled at her. 'I think it's a grand idea. It's the sort of thing Mark would have wanted to do for someone.'

Susan could not speak. She liked the idea. They had somehow managed to get through Mark's funeral. This time they would be celebrating his life.

The Christmas Ball was a success. At home together later that night Susan said, 'You know, the words that will stay with me the most came from one of his tutors, when he said that Mark had already achieved his goal. A soldier was what he'd always wanted to be.'

Peter reached for her hand. 'The ramblers suggested having an annual walk in his memory. We could call it "The Mark James Walk." I said I'd discuss it with you.'

'Yes, yes,' she said, 'but it must be his favourite walk: along the beach, close to the sea.'

At Midnight Mass, Peter and Susan held hands and watched the procession of chanting monks pass along the aisle. She felt Peter relax in the ancient church. Susan's grip on his hand slackened and she let her arm hang loose at her side. One day at a time, they had agreed. They were getting through it.

Epiphany

Carole Wilkinson

A
light
transforms
realisation.
Knowledge
released
inside
me.
Enlightenment,
awakening me.
To a journey,
Once unknown.
Thoughtfulness.
Clarity begins.
Perspective, life
now changing.
Where once, a
darkness dwelled,
A flickering flame
Of light dispels.
A profound, defining moment
Of revelation and light.

...

Grace Haddon

A cold cup of tea on the dining room table,
A neatly-wrapped present without any label.
A single odd sock that's missing its mate,
The everyday chore to remember the date.

Unreadable post-it notes stuck on the wall,
A folder of coursework just left in the hall.
Yesterday's breakfast: a stale bread roll,
My cat's big sad eyes at his empty food bowl.

A roadmap that no longer makes any sense,
A can of paint sitting by the old garden fence.
Footprints on the doormat where someone has stepped,
Sweaty sprints to work because I overslept.

A stranger who knows me, and keeps saying "hi",
A flytrap too thirsty to catch any flies.
A plate of spaghetti that's no longer hot,
I had a name for this poem –
I forgot.

Patience

Matty Kelsall

She rested her wrinkled hand on her husband's lap as they sat and stared through the windscreen and out over the seemingly-endless bright green Cheshire plains.

She smiled at him as he stared off into the distance. 'This really takes me back,' she said. 'Don't you feel the same?'

He batted her hand away, sending an empty sandwich wrapper and a heap of crumbs across the dashboard. 'No.'

She frowned. 'What's wrong, dear?'

'John Wayne,' he replied. 'That new John Wayne film is in the theatre tomorrow. Mummy won't take me. Will you, Grandma?'

She packed up the remains of the picnic, started the car and wound up the windows. 'Yes dear,' she murmured, 'I'll take you to see John Wayne tomorrow.'

He smiled as she released the handbrake and started up the car. 'Thanks, Grandma.'

'Anything for you, darling. Anything for you.'

Cover of the Book

Carole Wilkinson

Poised in the doorway of the café, I noticed the usual faces in there. Averting my eyes I slowly approached the counter, feeling eyes boring into me as I ordered my coffee. Most likely from the large man seated behind the counter. I'd seen him, always watching. Usually the young waitress or eyeing up and touching the older one every chance he got.

I shuddered as I made my way over to a table by the window, passing a middle-aged, bearded man, in hippy-style clothing with long beads dangling to his chest, seated in the corner. He was sat alone. He was always there, alone, until he spied a victim to foist himself onto. Probably a freeloader. Today that victim was a young man in tatty clothes, tattoos clearly visible on his neck and hands. They were deep in conversation. No doubt they had a lot in common, two freeloaders together. I breathed a sigh of relief that it wasn't going to be me he harassed.

I stared down at the carpet as I sank into my chair, scraps of food that had stained it over the years engraving discoloured patterns into it. Its musty smell mixing with the aroma of charred bacon that was wafting through from the kitchen as the door opened. The waitress approached with my coffee and placed it down.

'Thank you,' I whispered as I stared at it.

I held my breath as she hovered there a moment before turning to clear the table behind me.

Reaching into my pocket I pulled out a notebook, placing it on the table before picking up the mug. A self-help book I'd read stated that writing down your thoughts helped, but two months of writing and still no closer to peace. What did they know? Probably some rich bitch, without a care in the world, spouting bloody crap.

My eyes strayed from it to gaze out of the window. Why was I even here when the bridge was calling me? I stared as my grip tightened on the handle of the mug.

'You okay love?'

I wasn't his love. Why did people feel this need to offer synthetic sympathy? I had seen his reflection. I knew it was him, the freeloader. My eyes closed.

'Mind if I sit down?'

I hadn't come in the café for company. As I opened my eyes, he'd already seated himself. I turned my head to scowl at him.

He smiled. 'It's a lovely day.'

I automatically glanced back at the window. The sun was shining, mocking, casting shadows that disappeared as the clouds obscured its view. If there were any justice it would disappear, permanently. Cast everywhere into darkness. I looked back at his smiling face. He obviously didn't have any problems, unless it was that fake smile we often portray to the world?

I put down my mug as his eyes strayed to my notebook. I snatched it up, it was mine. My private thoughts and not his to snoop and ridicule.

'Sorry, didn't mean to pry,' he said as he glanced at it. 'I'm Brian, by the way. I've seen you in here a few times. If you don't mind me saying so, you look like you could do with some cheering up.'

Cheering up? I glared, loathing every inch of him. Six months ago I wouldn't have taken such an immediately strong dislike to him. But that was then. Right now I wanted the floor to suck him down and then spew his rotten corpse into the street for the scavengers to pick at. The world was full of them, picking at you till you ceased to exist.

I sighed. 'Really?'

'Oh, so you do speak.'

'What's it to you?' I sat back. 'Look... I don't mean to be rude, but...'

He laughed and I turned my head away. 'But you will be anyway. No doubt you want me to go and sit somewhere else. You want to be left alone to sip your coffee, and me and the world can go to Hell.'

My head turned back. 'You read minds then?'

'Ah, the lady has a sense of humour I see. Not much, but it's there all the same.'

'Now look!'

'I am looking. You're an attractive young woman, well-dressed, nice manners, at least to the staff.' He leant forward slightly. I jerked back away from him.

'I've seen you come in here. You order your coffee and sit at the same table, staring out of the window for a while and writing in there.' He gestured towards my notebook. 'You have a look of torment and often sadness about you.'

My hands felt clammy as I held the notebook tighter, fearing that he would snatch it, clasping it to my chest as a barrier between us.

He placed his elbows on the red tablecloth and clasped his hands together to rest his chin. 'I'm in the business of helping people and I'm offering you my services.'

I'd had enough of his invasion, his arrogance. I took a deep breath and glared into his eyes. 'I'm fine, I don't need your help.'

Blue eyes captured mine, ripping through my barriers and invading me. His face changed to one of concern.

Oh my God he knows! My breathing quickened as I tore free of his gaze.

'Your eyes tell me a different story. Did you know that eyes are the windows to your soul?'

I did now!

'So tell me. What do you think about as you sit looking out?'

I felt momentary relief that maybe he hadn't seen the truth. I wrapped myself in protective numbness, resigning myself to his interrogation as my breathing slowed and raised my eyebrows. 'Do you really want to know?'

He moved his large frame back against the chair, nodding. 'Yes, actually I do.'

I expected his eyes to flicker, that slight movement to signal a lie. For a moment I thought I saw concern, but most likely it was nosy curiosity and nothing more. Well he was out of luck, he wasn't going to get his gossip. It was my secret.

I thought for a moment. 'I watch people and write down what I see. How corrupt they are, doing each other down day after day. No-one cares. Life! A living Hell for most. People abused daily. There's no good in this world. Why are we even born?' I drifted into my solitary world and was startled by his response.

'We are born to live. We laugh, we cry and we love. Forever searching on our journey. We learn as we go. They say that the good we do for others comes back to us tenfold. I strongly believe this to be true.'

Oh God! A bloody preacher!

'What a crock of shit! I've always been a good person, I help others and what did that get me? The world is full of vile creatures.'

I looked around searching for a victim to spout against. 'That man there.'

I nodded in the direction of the middle-aged man sat behind the serving counter, reading his newspaper. 'He sits there every day and never lifts a finger, unless it's to slap that waitress on the bum.' I inclined my head towards her. 'He's constantly touching her. Doesn't he realise it's illegal to do that? She probably needs the work and men like him just take advantage.'

I leaned forward slightly. 'And the young waitress with the facial scar, he's winking and calling her beautiful and gorgeous all the time. You can tell she's uncomfortable by the way she hangs her head every time. They could have him done for sexual harassment, you know. He's a disgusting letch. She's young enough to be his daughter.'

I stopped, expecting a response, some form of agreement, but instead was confronted with a bemused expression. What did I expect? He was a man after all. They were all the same. Take what they wanted. No didn't mean anything to them. My hand gripped the notebook harder to my chest. The numbness I'd felt for so long now a simmering rage needing release. My eyes darted around the room as I pushed back my chair. I had to escape.

'Why don't you just leave me alone? I didn't ask for your help.'

'Oh, but you did.'

I stared. The nerve of the man. 'When?'

He leant further forward. 'Every time you stepped across the threshold of the café. As I said earlier, I've been watching you. Every day these past two months, the same ritual.'

He gestured towards the green metal bridge that had been my constant companion.

'You go to that bridge and grip the rail tightly as you look down at the water, sometimes for as long as a couple of hours. You turn away, cross over to here and step through this door. Those that want help are guided here, those that don't...' He shrugged.

I sank back in the chair and looked at the bridge, confused. His next words caused me to sink further.

'The man you speak of is Colin, my manager. He chose the door five years ago when he nearly lost his wife and daughter… The ones you just mentioned.'

I gasped, my hand going to my mouth.

'Their car spun out of control, not his fault, but, as he was driving he blamed himself. His wife lying in a coma and him not knowing whether she'd live or die and if she did, then what sort of life would she have? His daughter needed surgery to repair her damaged face. The surgeons were very skilled, but the scars… Well you've seen them. Consumed with guilt he thought to go to the water, as you have. It would all be over. But, like you, he was guided here…'

My hands covered my face as he continued.

'…He touches his wife constantly because he thought he would never be able to hold her again, so he treasures every touch, every look and every word that they share together. He sees the scars on his daughter's face, a constant reminder to them both, and tells her every moment of the day how beautiful she is. Beauty comes from within and her soul is beautiful. It always will be to those with eyes that truly see. And as for Colin? His legs were crushed on impact, mobility is limited and extremely painful. So he does the best he can and helps by being here and supporting those that he loves and cares for, above all else.'

He leaned forward to take my hands away from my crimsoned face. I was glad that the glaze of unshed tears obstructed my vision of what must surely be a look of disgust from him. I felt soft cotton pressed into my hand as he spoke.

'Many people walk the bridge, looking for answers or an end. As I said earlier, my name is Brian and I'm in the business of helping people. What can I do for you today?'

I raised the cloth to my eyes as the tears escaped. I searched his face for a clue, something to show me that I couldn't trust him. His eyes once again captured me, penetrating. I was thankful for a movement out of the corner of my eye breaking his gaze. My head turned to see a young woman, coat draped over her arm.

'Sorry to interrupt, but I just wanted to say goodbye before I left,' she said as she looked expectantly at Brian.

'No problem, Brenda.' He smiled as he rose to his feet, towering above her, a slender girl who couldn't have been more than five foot tall. His arms encircled her as she stepped towards him.

Her face looked up at him, smiling. 'I pick the keys up in an hour and just wanted to say thank you. Finally, a place I can call mine and I owe it all to you. I'll always be grateful and I'll never forget what you've done for me.' She squeezed before moving away.

'It was my pleasure and don't forget, it was you that took those first steps. Time to move forward, don't look back. You'll have a wonderful life, I'm sure.'

'Me too. Take care of yourself and thanks again.' She smiled and made her way to the door, pausing to wave as she left the café.

Brian seated himself once again. 'Well it looks like I have a vacancy for a new waitress.' He looked at me expectantly.

I looked over at the old bridge for a moment, noted its peeling paint and unwelcoming steel, then back at Brian. Could this be my first tentative step? I took a deep breath.

'My name is Amy and I'd like to apply.'

He smiled. 'A wise decision, Amy.'

The Clouds Are White Horses

Anouschka Greenwood

When Randall Lamb was twelve he was in love. His complete world revolved around her. Even as he lay on his back in the vastness of the meadow he could feel the Earth below him spinning, hurtling around the sun. He dug his fingers into the ground until the soil crept underneath his bitten nails.

Randall rolled his head so he faced the east breeze. He squinted as he gazed at the view of his homeland. Blades of grass, one centimetre tall. That emerald green, and the sort that brushed softly against the soles of your feet and slightly tickled your heels. Extending for miles. The reds and yellows of tulip heads protruded and bloomed in the gentle heat. A crystal stream ran through the centre in gentle curves and the water lapped on the rocks, on the banks, watering the grass without causing mud and bog.

Edible berries grew in families. The deepest of purples, clinging together in protection from the swift breeze that rippled across the land. The houses' exteriors were painted in a pastel rainbow with matching front doors. Windows were propped open and washing was hung out onto balconies to dry in the midday sun. A perfect, orange circle sat in the centre of the soft, blue sky.

He closed his eyes and thought of her. Her scraped knees and the gap in her teeth. How her plaits bounced on her scrawny shoulders when she ran and how her breath smelt like tomato soup.

'Are you asleep?' Randall felt a soft kick at his elbow. He jerked his neck and saw her. Those five large freckles on her left cheek, and the permanent line between her eyebrows. 'Oi!'

'Heidi.' Randall's head fell back on the grass. He could feel his heart racing. Feel it racing faster than the Earth was turning. He rubbed together the heels of his trainers and she sat cross-legged next to him. She plucked at the perfect blades and rolled them between her fingers. Randall turned onto his side to face her. 'What're you doing here?'

'Wanted somewhere peaceful to do my homework,' Heidi replied, waving a crumpled sheet of paper. She tried to smooth the paper down on the ground in front of her, pulled a pencil from behind her ear and began scribbling notes.

'You're always working,' Randall sighed.

'Am not!'

'You so are.'

Heidi watched him, stopping only when her eyelids forced her to blink. She removed her hand from her homework and Randall's heart stopped as the paper floated across his view and became a part of his landscape.

'You're gonna get in so much trouble.' But Randall couldn't help but smile.

'Don't do it either,' Heidi said. 'We can get in trouble together.'

Randall liked that idea and nodded. 'I'll rip it up.' But as he said it, and as she laughed a laugh he wished he could hear forever, he vowed that upon his return home, he would find that homework and save it. Put it in a box and forever remember it as the reason he could spend more time with Heidi. The best homework he had ever been given.

Randall grew aware of Heidi's movement in his peripheral vision, and her lying down beside him, but he couldn't let himself take his eyes off the sky.

'Mum always took me cloud watching,' Heidi's voice was soft and Randall pretended the breeze on his face was the breath from her words. 'We used to lie back and look at the sky, and she used to point and say things like, "Gosh –

don't those clouds look like white horses," and obviously they didn't but I used to pretend. Pretend I agreed with her. Pretend the clouds are white horses. Adults like it when you do that, have you noticed? They love to pretend, and love it when you suck it right up and believe them. Pretending. That's what they call it anyway. Santa Claus, the Tooth Fairy, the clouds. It's all just lies. But because they're old it's okay for them to lie.'

'We'll be old one day. Then we can do the same.'

'I won't,' Heidi insisted. 'I'll tell the truth. The clouds will be clouds, and Santa Claus will never exist.'

Randall couldn't help but laugh.

'It's not funny.'

'You're funny,' he said, turning to look at her.

'You're funny-looking.' Heidi looked back at him, reaching out her hand gently. The side of their hands grazed past each other, and they let their pinkies intertwine.

'If there was no Santa you would never have had any presents at Christmas.'

'Oh well,' Heidi shrugged. 'The dinner is the best bit.'

Randall laughed again. 'I'd get you a present, anyway.'

Heidi simply smiled. The smile that created cracks in her lips and showed the toothy gap Randall adored. In its glow, Randall hadn't noticed the sun vanishing behind the clouds.

'I have to get back. It looks like it's going to rain,' Heidi sighed. 'And I don't have a coat.' She jumped to her feet, ankles shaking under the weight of her own gangly body. Randall didn't move.

'I miss you already.'

'Of course you do.' Heidi leaped over him and ran, downstream, into the village with her arms flailing alongside her. Randall watched her until she got smaller and smaller; until she was no bigger than the heads of the red and yellow tulips. Until she was invisible to the naked eye. And until she had gone.

The Inspirer

Kwaku Asafu-Agyei

When I found assignments
Difficult to comprehend you
Always had patience to break
Down the assignments in a way
I could gravitate.

Times when you were seriously
Ill; you still made an effort to show
Up to lectures to educate the class;
For you cared about your students;
And as a student of yours this spoke
Volumes to me.

At first I knew I could string two words
Together; but you made me a writer.
Now you are gone; and there is a gap
At university; I guess God needed a
Star; so he took you.

So this limerick is for you David Kershaw
As my tutor; just to say thank you for
What you taught me; and if I make
through this final of Uni; you will be
one of the reasons
Why.

David you are gone; but you will never be
Forgotten; may your soul rest in perfect
Peace. You are missed.

Meet The Crew!

In between playing the hero in Dungeons & Dragons and brushing up on his Japanese, **Dale Cross** enjoys writing high fantasy stories filled with dragons, spells and swords. After graduating from his creative and professional writing course, he hopes to spend the rest of his days teaching English in Japan.

Sarah Daoud got the writing bug as a child and eventually realised that screenwriting was it for her. She recently wrote the winning scene for Sketch Up, a local TV show. The scene, *Keeping Shop*, has since been made into a short film. Sarah is now considering world domination. Once she's finished uni of course. And gotten a job. And made some money.

When not writing poetry or prose with an overabundance of imagery, **Anouschka Greenwood** works at a jewellery shop to fund her travels around the world. She loves historical novels, memoirs and romantic films. A great cook if you like mushrooms.

When she isn't hunting Skyrim trophies or talking to her carnivorous plant collection, **Grace Haddon** writes fantasy stories. In 2015 she won Malorie Blackman's *Project Remix* competition and is a regular writer for Leicester charity initiative *The Big Care Write-Up*. She was the editor of *Vices and Virtues.* Her ambition is to one day own a TARDIS and become a time-traveller. But failing that, a novelist will do. www.gracehaddon.com

Matty Kelsall is a fantasy writer and poet from an ancient Viking island. His writing is tight, his wit is quick, and he's never afraid to change up his style.

Carys Kitchin - the most unappreciated writer in the "you are shit" category. She writes whatever she feels even if it makes no sense. Read her stuff and embrace the confusion.

Known online as ThatGingerBrit (except on twitter, where it was taken), **Greg Morrison** has been described as "pretentious" "insufferable" and "somehow still likable" which he thinks is the perfect description of every good writer. His life consists entirely of writing about, reading about, and thinking about superheroes.
twitter - @gregamiah

Isabel Payne is a third-year part-time mature student at Nottingham University. She often writes short stories set in war zones or in the crime genre. She has acted in amateur stage productions and written a script for a stage play, which she hopes to get published.

Mick Powis enjoys reading war and crime novels. He is currently working on a crime/thriller novel, which he hopes to publish in the future. Drawing on his experience of twenty years in the Civil Service to give an authentic voice to his writing.

Carole Wilkinson is currently in her second year at university. She expresses her experiences of life and relationships through poetry and short stories. Her love of fantasy has led her to working on a series of adventure novels for children, which she aims to publish in the near future.